SLEEPING FIRES

A NOVEL

GERTRUDE ATHERTON

1st WORLD
LIBRARY
Literary Society

Sleeping Fires

Gertrude Atherton

© 1st World Library – Literary Society, 2004
PO Box 2211
Fairfield, IA 52556
www.1stworldlibrary.org
First Edition

LCCN: 2004195302

Softcover ISBN: 1-4218-0133-7
Hardcover ISBN: 1-4218-0033-0
eBook ISBN: 1-4218-0233-3

Purchase *"Sleeping Fires"*
as a traditional bound book at:
www.1stWorldLibrary.org/purchase.asp?ISBN=1-4218-0133-7

1st World Library Literary Society is a nonprofit organization dedicated to promoting literacy by:

- Creating a free internet library accessible from any computer worldwide.
- Hosting writing competitions and offering book publishing scholarships.

Readers interested in supporting literacy
through sponsorship, donations or
membership please contact:
literacy@1stworldlibrary.org
Check us out at: www.1stworldlibrary.ORG
and start downloading free ebooks today.

Sleeping Fires
contributed by Tim, Ed & Rodney
in support of
1st World Library Literary Society

I

There was no Burlingame in the Sixties, the Western Addition was a desert of sand dunes and the goats gambolled through the rocky gulches of Nob Hill. But San Francisco had its Rincon Hill and South Park, Howard and Fulsom and Harrison Streets, coldly aloof from the tumultuous hot heart of the City north of Market Street.

In this residence section the sidewalks were also wooden and uneven and the streets muddy in winter and dusty in summer, but the houses, some of which had "come round the Horn," were large, simple, and stately. Those on the three long streets had deep gardens before them, with willow trees and oaks above the flower beds, quaint ugly statues, and fountains that were sometimes dry. The narrower houses of South Park crowded one another about the oval enclosure and their common garden was the smaller oval of green and roses.

On Rincon Hill the architecture was more varied and the houses that covered all sides of the hill were surrounded by high-walled gardens whose heavy bushes of Castilian roses were the only reminder in this already modern San Francisco of the Spain that had made California a land of romance for nearly a century; the last resting place on this planet of the

Spirit of Arcadia ere she vanished into space before the gold-seekers.

On far-flung heights beyond the business section crowded between Market and Clay Streets were isolated mansions, built by prescient men whose belief in the rapid growth of the city to the north and west was justified in due course, but which sheltered at present amiable and sociable ladies who lamented their separation by vast spaces from that aristocratic quarter of the south.

But they had their carriages, and on a certain Sunday afternoon several of these arks drawn by stout horses might have been seen crawling fearfully down the steep hills or floundering through the sand until they reached Market Street; when the coachmen cracked their whips, the horses trotted briskly, and shortly after began toascend Rincon Hill.

Mrs. Hunt McLane, the social dictator of her little world, had recently moved from South Park into a large house on Rincon Hill that had been built by an eminent citizen who had lost his fortune as abruptly as he had made it; and this was her housewarming. It was safe to say that her rooms would be crowded, and not merely because her Sunday receptions were the most important minor functions in San Francisco: it was possible that Dr. Talbot and his bride would be there. And if he were not it might be long before curiosity would be gratified by even a glance at the stranger; the doctor detested the theatre and had engaged a suite at the Occidental Hotel with a private dining-room.

Several weeks before a solemn conclave had been held at Mrs. McLane's house in South Park. Mrs. Abbott was there and Mrs. Ballinger, both second only to Mrs. McLane in social leadership; Mrs. Montgomery, Mrs. Brannan, and other women whose power was rooted in the Fifties; Maria and Sally Ballinger, Marguerite McLane, and Guadalupe Hathaway, whose blue large talking Spanish eyes had made her the belle of many seasons: all met to discuss the disquieting news of the marriage in Boston of the most popular and fashionable doctor in San Francisco, Howard Talbot. He had gone East for a vacation, and soon after had sent them a bald announcement of his marriage to one Madeleine Chilton of Boston.

Many high hopes had centered in Dr. Talbot. He was only forty, good-looking, with exuberant spirits, and well on the road to fortune. He had been surrounded in San Francisco by beautiful and vivacious girls, but had always proclaimed himself a man's man, avowed he had seen too much of babies and "blues," and should die an old bachelor. Besides he loved them all; when he did not damn them roundly, which he sometimes did to their secret delight.

And now he not only had affronted them by marrying some one he probably never had seen before, but he had taken a Northern wife; he had not even had the grace to go to his native South, if he must marry an outsider; he had gone to Boston - of all places!

San Francisco Society in the Sixties was composed almost entirely of Southerners. Even before the war it had been difficult for a Northerner to obtain entrance to that sacrosanct circle; the exceptions were due to sheer personality. Southerners were aristocrats. The North was plebeian. That was final. Since the war, Victorious North continued to admit defeat in

California. The South had its last stronghold in San Francisco, and held it, haughty, unconquered, inflexible.

That Dr. Talbot, who was on a family footing in every home in San Francisco, should have placed his friends in such a delicate position (to say nothing of shattered hopes) was voted an outrage, and at Mrs. McLane's on that former Sunday afternoon, there had been no pretence at indifference. The subject was thoroughly discussed. It was possible that the creature might not even be a lady. Had any one ever heard of a Boston family named Chilton? No one had. They knew nothing of Boston and cared less. But the best would be bad enough.

It was more likely however that the doctor had married some obscure person with nothing in her favor but youth, or a widow of practiced wiles, or - horrid thought - a divorcee.

He had always been absurdly liberal in spite of his blue Southern blood; and a man's man wandering alone at the age of forty was almost foredoomed to disaster. No doubt the poor man had been homesick and lonesome.

Should they receive her or should they not? If not, would they lose their doctor. He would never speak to one of them again if they insulted his wife. But a Bostonian, a possible nobody! And homely, of course. Angular. Who had ever heard of a pretty woman raised on beans, codfish, and pie for breakfast?

Finally Mrs. McLane had announced that she should not make up her mind until the couple arrived and she sat in judgment upon the woman personally. She would call the day after they docked in San Francisco. If, by any chance, the woman were presentable, dressed herself with some regard to the fashion (which was more than Mrs. Abbott and Guadalupe Hathaway did), and had sufficient tact to avoid the subject of the war, she would stand sponsor and invite her to the first reception in the house on Rincon Hill.

"But if not," she said grimly - "well, not even for Howard Talbot's sake will I receive a woman who is not a lady, or who has been divorced. In this wild city we are a class apart, above. No loose fish enters our quiet bay. Only by the most rigid code and watchfulness have we formed and preserved a society similar to that we were accustomed to in the old South. If we lowered our barriers we should be submerged. If Howard Talbot has married a woman we do not find ourselves able to associate with in this intimate little society out here on the edge of the world, he will have to go."

II

Mrs. McLane had called on Mrs. Talbot. That was known to all San Francisco, for her carriage had stood in front of the Occidental Hotel for an hour. Kind friends had called to offer their services in setting the new house in order, but were dismissed at the door with the brief announcement that Mrs. McLane was having the blues. No one wasted time on a second effort to gossip with their leader; it was known that just so often Mrs. McLane drew down the blinds, informed her household that she was not to be disturbed, disposed herself on the sofa with her back to the room and indulged in the luxury of blues for three days. She took no nourishment but milk and broth and spoke to no one. Today this would be a rest cure and was equally beneficial. When the attack was over Mrs. McLane would arise with a clear complexion, serene nerves, and renewed strength for social duties. Her friends knew that her retirement on this occasion was timed to finish on the morning of her reception and had not the least misgiving that her doors would still be closed.

The great double parlors of her new mansion were thrown into one and the simple furniture covered with gray rep was pushed against soft gray walls hung with several old portraits in oil, ferrotypes and silhouettes. A magnificent crystal chandelier depended from the high and lightly frescoed ceiling and there were side brackets beside the doors and the low mantel piece. Mrs. McLane may not have been able to achieve beauty with the aid of the San Francisco shops, but at least she had managed to give her rooms a severe and stately simplicity, vastly different from the helpless surrenders of her friends to mid-victorian deformities.

The rooms filled early. Mrs. McLane stood before the north windows receiving her friends with her usual brilliant smile, her manner of high dignity and sweet cordiality. She was a majestic figure in spite of her short stature and increasing curves, for the majesty was within and her head above a flat back had a lofty poise. She wore her prematurely white hair in a tall pompadour, and this with the rich velvets she affected, ample and long, made her look like a French marquise of the eighteenth century, stepped down from the canvas. The effect was by no means accidental. Mrs. McLane's grandmother had been French and she resembled her.

Her hoopskirt was small, but the other women were inclined to the extreme of the fashion; as they saw it in the Godey's Lady's Book they or their dressmakers subscribed to. Their handsome gowns spread widely and the rooms hardly could have seemed to sway and undulate more if an earthquake had rocked it. The older women wore small bonnets and cashmere shawls, lace collars and cameos, the younger fichus and small flat hats above their "waterfalls" or curled chignons. The husbands had retired with Mr. McLane to the smoking room, but there were many beaux present, equally expectant when not too absorbed.

Unlike as a reception of that day was in background

and costumes from the refinements of modern art and taste, it possessed one contrast that was wholly to its advantage. Its men were gentlemen and the sons and grandsons of gentlemen. To no one city has there ever been such an emigration of men of good family as to San Francisco in the Fifties and Sixties. Ambitious to push ahead in politics or the professions and appreciating the immediate opportunities of the new and famous city, or left with an insufficient inheritance (particularly after the war) and ashamed to work in communities where no gentleman had ever worked, they had set sail with a few hundreds to a land where a man, if he did not occupy himself lucratively, was unfit for the society of enterprising citizens.

Few had come in time for the gold diggings, but all, unless they had disappeared into the hot insatiable maw of the wicked little city, had succeeded in one field or another; and these, in their dandified clothes, made a fine appearance at fashionable gatherings. If they took up less room than the women they certainly were more decorative.

Dr. Talbot and his wife had not arrived. To all eager questions Mrs. McLane merely replied that "they" would "be here." She had the dramatic instinct of the true leader and had commanded the doctor not to bring his bride before four o'clock. The reception began at three. They should have an entrance. But Mrs. Abbott, a lady of three chins and an eagle eye, who had clung for twenty-five years to black satin and bugles, was too persistent to be denied. She extracted the information that the Bostonian had sent her own furniture by a previous steamer and that her drawing room was graceful, French, and exquisite.

At ten minutes after the hour the buzz and chatter stopped abruptly and every face was turned, every neck craned toward the door. The colored butler had announced with a grand flourish:

"Dr. and Mrs. Talbot."

The doctor looked as rubicund, as jovial, as cynical as ever. But few cast him more than a passing glance. Then they gave an audible gasp, induced by an ingenuous compound of amazement, disappointment, and admiration. They had been prepared to forgive, to endure, to make every allowance. The poor thing could no more help being plain and dowdy than born in Boston, and as their leader had satisfied herself that she "would do," they would never let her know how deeply they deplored her disabilities.

But they found nothing to deplore but the agonizing necessity for immediate readjustment. Mrs. Talbot was unquestionably a product of the best society. The South could have done no better. She was tall and supple and self-possessed. She was exquisitely dressed in dark blue velvet with a high collar of point lace tapering almost to her bust, and revealing a long white throat clasped at the base by a string of pearls. On her head, as proudly poised as Mrs. McLane's, was a blue velvet hat, higher in the crown than the prevailing fashion, rolled up on one side and trimmed only with a drooping gray feather. And her figure, her face, her profile! The young men crowded forward more swiftly than the still almost paralyzed women. She was no more than twenty. Her skin was as white as the San Francisco fogs, her lips were scarlet, her cheeks pink, her hair and eyes a bright golden brown. Her features were delicate and regular, the mouth not too small, curved and sensitive; her refinement was almost excessive. Oh, she was "high-toned," no doubt of that! As she moved forward and stood in front of Mrs. McLane, or acknowledged introductions to those that stood near, the women gave another gasp, this time of consternation. She wore neither hoop-skirt nor crinoline. Could it be that the most elegant fashion ever invented had been discarded by Paris? Or was this lovely creature of surpassing elegance, a law unto herself?

Her skirt was full but straight and did not disguise the lines of her graceful figure; above her small waist it fitted as closely as a riding habit. She was even more *becomingly* dressed than any woman in the room. Mrs. Abbott, who was given to primitive sounds, snorted. Maria Ballinger, whose finely developed figure might as well have been the trunk of a tree, sniffed. Her sister Sally almost danced with excitement, and even Miss Hathaway straightened her fichu. Mrs. Ballinger, who had been the belle of Richmond and was still adjudged the handsomest woman in San Francisco, lifted the eyebrows to which sonnets had been written with an air of haughty resignation; but made up her mind to abate her scorn of the North and order her gowns from New York hereafter.

But the San Franciscans on the whole were an amiable people and they were sometimes conscious of their isolation; in a few moments they felt a pleasant titillation of the nerves, as if the great world they might never see again had sent them one of her most precious gifts.

They all met her in the course of the afternoon. She was sweet and gracious, but although there was not a hint of embarrassment she made no attempt to shine, and they liked her the better for that. The young men soon discovered they could make no impression on this lovely importation, for her eyes strayed constantly to her husband; until he disappeared in search of cronies, whiskey, and a cigar: then she looked depressed for a moment, but gave a still closer attention to the women about her.

In love with her husband but a woman-of-the-world. Manners as fine as Mrs. McLane's, but too aloof and sensitive to care for leadership. She had made the grand tour in Europe, they discovered, and enjoyed a season in Washington. She should continue to live at the Occidental Hotel as her husband would be out so much at night and she was rather timid. And she was bright, unaffected, responsive. Could anything be more reassuring? There was nothing to be apprehended by the socially ambitious, the proud housewives, or those prudent dames whose amours were conducted with such secrecy that they might too easily be supplanted by a predatory coquette. The girls drew little unconscious sighs of relief. Sally Ballinger vowed she would become her intimate friend, Sibyl Geary that she would copy her gowns. Mrs. Abbott succumbed. In short they all took her to their hearts. She was one of them from that time forth and the reign of crinoline was over.

III

The Talbots remained to supper and arrived at the Occidental Hotel at the dissipated hour of half past nine. As they entered their suite the bride took her sweeping skirts in either hand and executed a pas seul down the long parlor.

"I was a success!" she cried. "You were proud of me. I could see it. And even at the table, although I talked nearly all the time to Mr. McLane, I never mentioned a book."

She danced over and threw her arms about his neck. "Say you were proud of me. I'd love to hear it."

He gave her a bear-like hug. "Of course. You are the prettiest and the most animated woman in San Francisco, and that's saying a good deal. And I've given them all a mighty surprise."

"I believe that is the longest compliment you ever paid me - and because I made a good impression on some one else. What irony!"

She pouted charmingly, but her eyes were wistful. "Now sit down and talk to me. I've scarcely seen you since we arrived."

Gertrude Atherton

"Oh! Remember you are married to this old ruffian. You'll see enough of me in the next thirty or forty years. Run to bed and get your beauty sleep. I promised to go to the Union Club."

"The Club? You went to the Club last night and the night before and the night before that. Every night since we arrived -"

"I haven't seen half my old cronies yet and they are waiting for a good old poker game. Sleep is what you want after such an exciting day. Remember, I doctor the nerves of all the women in San Francisco and this is a hard climate on nerves. Wonder more women don't go to the devil."

He kissed her again and escaped hurriedly. Those were the days when women wept facilely, "swooned," inhaled hartshorn, calmed themselves with sal volatile, and even went into hysterics upon slight provocation. Madeleine Talbot merely wept. She believed herself to be profoundly in love with her jovial magnetic if rather rough husband. He was so different from the correct reserved men she had been associated with during her anchored life in Boston. In Washington she had met only the staid old families, and senators of a benignant formality. In Europe she had run across no one she knew who might have introduced her to interesting foreigners, and Mrs. Chilton would as willingly have caressed a tiger as spoken to a stranger no matter how prepossessing. Howard Talbot, whom she had met at the house of a common friend, had taken her by storm. Her family had disapproved, not only because he was by birth a Southerner, but for the same reason that had attracted their Madeleine. He was entirely too different. Moreover, he would take her to a barbarous country where there was no Society and people dared not venture into the streets lest they be shot. But she had overruled them and been very happy - at times. He was charming and adorable and it was manifest that for him no other woman existed.

But she could not flatter herself that she was indispensable. He openly preferred the society of men, and during that interminable sea voyage she had seen little of him save at the table or when he came to their stateroom late at night. For her mind he appeared to have a good-natured masculine contempt. He talked to her as he would to a fascinating little girl. If he cared for mental recreation he found it in men.

She went into her bedroom and bathed her eyes with eau de cologne. At least he had given her no cause for jealousy. That was one compensation. And a wise married friend had told her that the only way to manage a husband was to give him his head and never to indulge in the luxury of reproaches. She was sorry she had forgotten herself tonight.

Gertrude Atherton

IV

Dr. Talbot had confided to Mrs. McLane that his wife was inclined to be a bas bleu and he wanted her broken of an unfeminine love of books. Mrs. McLane, who knew that a reputation for bookishness would be fatal in a community that regarded "Lucile" as a great poem and read little but the few novels that drifted their way (or the continued stories in Godey's Lady's Book), promised him that Madeleine's intellectual aspirations should be submerged in the social gaieties of the season.

She kept her word. Dinners, receptions, luncheons, theatre parties, in honor of the bride, followed in rapid succession, and when all had entertained her, the less personal invitations followed as rapidly. Her popularity was not founded on novelty.

No girl in her first season had ever enjoyed herself more naively and she brought to every entertainment eager sparkling eyes and dancing feet that never tired. She became the "reigning toast." At parties she was surrounded by a bevy of admirers or forced to divide her dances; for it was soon patent there was no jealousy in Talbot's composition and that he took an equally naive pride in his wife's success. When alone with women she was quite as animated and interested, and, moreover, invited them to copy her gowns. Some had been made in Paris, others in New York. The local dressmakers felt the stirrings of ambition, and the shops sent for a more varied assortment of fabrics.

Madeleine Talbot at this time was very happy, or, at least, too busy to recall her earlier dreams of happiness. The whole-hearted devotion to gaiety of this stranded little community, its elegance, despite its limitations, its unbounded hospitality to all within its guarded portals, its very absence of intellectual criticism, made the formal life of her brief past appear dull and drab in the retrospect. The spirit of Puritanism seemed to have lost heart in those trackless wastes between the Atlantic and the Pacific and turned back. True, the moral code was rigid (on the surface); but far from too much enjoyment of life, of quaffing eagerly at the brimming cup, being sinful, they would have held it to be a far greater sin not to have accepted all that the genius of San Francisco so lavishly provided.

Wildness and recklessness were in the air, the night life of San Francisco was probably the maddest in the world; nor did the gambling houses close their doors by day, nor the women of Dupont Street cease from leering through their shuttered windows; a city born in delirium and nourished on crime, whose very atmosphere was electrified and whose very foundations were restless, would take a quarter of a century at least to manufacture a decent thick surface of conventionality, and its self-conscious respectable wing could no more escape its spirit than its fogs and winds. But evil excitement was tempered to irresponsible gaiety, a constant whirl of innocent pleasures. When the spirit passed the portals untempered, and drove women too highly-strung, too unhappy, or too easily bored, to the divorce courts, to drink, or to

Gertrude Atherton

reckless adventure, they were summarily dropped. No woman, however guiltless, could divorce her husband and remain a member of that vigilant court. It was all or nothing. If a married woman were clever enough to take a lover undetected and merely furnish interesting surmise, there was no attempt to ferret out and punish her; for no society can exist without gossip.

But none centered about Madeleine Talbot. Her little coquetries were impartial and her devotion to her husband was patent to the most infatuated eye. Life was made very pleasant for her. Howard, during that first winter, accompanied her to all the dinners and parties, and she gave several entertainments in her large suite at the Occidental Hotel. Sally Ballinger was a lively companion for the mornings and was as devoted a friend as youth could demand. Mrs. Abbott petted her, and Mrs. Ballinger forgot that she had been born in Boston.

When it was discovered that she had a sweet lyric soprano, charmingly cultivated, her popularity winged another flight; San Francisco from its earliest days was musical, and she made a brilliant success as La Belle Helene in the amateur light opera company organized by Mrs. McLane. It was rarely that she spent an evening alone, and the cases of books she had brought from Boston remained in the cellars of the Hotel.

V

Society went to the country to escape the screaming winds and dust clouds of summer. A few had built country houses, the rest found abundant amusement at the hotels of The Geysers, Warm Springs and Congress Springs, taking the waters dutifully.

As the city was constantly swept by epidemics Dr. Talbot rarely left his post for even a few days' shooting, and Madeleine remained with him as a matter of course. Moreover, she hoped for occasional long evenings with her husband and the opportunity to convince him that her companionship was more satisfying than that of his friends at the Club. She had not renounced the design of gradually converting him to her own love of literature, and pictured delightful hours during which they would discuss the world's masterpieces together.

But he merely hooted amiably and pinched her cheeks when she approached the subject tentatively. He was infernally over-worked and unless he had a few hours' relaxation at the Club he would be unfit for duty on the morrow. She was his heart's delight, the prettiest wife in San Francisco; he worked the better because she was always lovely at the breakfast table and he could look forward to a brief dinner in her always radiant company. Thank God, she never had the blues nor carried a bottle of smelling salts about with her. And she hadn't a nerve in her body! God! How he did hate women's nerves. No, she was a model wife and he adored her unceasingly. But companionship? When she timidly uttered the word, he first stared uncomprehendingly, then burst into loud laughter.

"Men don't find companionship in women, my dear. If they pretend to they're after something else. Take the word of an old stager for that. Of course there is no such thing as companionship among women as men understand the term, but you have Society, which is really all you want. Yearnings are merely a symptom of those accursed nerves. For God's sake forget them. Flirt all you choose - there are plenty of men in town; have them in for dinner if you like - but if any of those young bucks talks companionship to you put up your guard or come and tell me. I'll settle his hash."

"I don't want the companionship of any other man, but I'd like yours."

"You don't know how lucky you are. You have all of me you could stand. Three or four long evenings - well, we'd yawn in each other's faces and go to bed. A bull but true enough."

"Then I think I'll have the books unpacked, not only those I brought, but the new case papa sent to me. I have lost the resource of Society for several months, and I do not care to have men here after you have gone. That would mean gossip."

"You are above gossip and I prefer the men to the books. You'll ruin your pretty eyes, and you had the makings of a fine bluestocking when I rescued you. A successful woman - with her husband and with Society - has only sparkling shallows in her pretty little head. Now, I must run. I really shouldn't have come all the way up here for lunch."

Madeleine wandered aimlessly to the window and looked down at the scurrying throngs on Montgomery Street. There were few women. The men bent against the wind, clutching at their hats, or chasing them along the uneven wooden sidewalks, tripping perhaps on a loose board. There were tiny whirlwinds of dust in the unpaved streets. The bustling little city that Madeleine had thought so picturesque in its novelty suddenly lost its glamour. It looked as if parts of it had been flung together in a night between solid blocks imported from the older communities; so furious was the desire to achieve immediate wealth there were only three or four buildings of architectural beauty in the city. The shop windows on Montgomery Street were attractive with the wares of Paris, but Madeleine coveted nothing in San Francisco.

She thought of Boston, New York, Washington, Europe, and for a moment nostalgia overwhelmed her. If Howard would only take her home for a visit! Alas! he was as little likely to do that as to give her the companionship she craved.

But she had no intention of taking refuge in tears. Nor would she stay at home and mope. Her friends were out of town. She made up her mind to go for a walk, although she hardly knew where to go. Between mud and dust and hills, walking was not popular in San Francisco. However, there might be some excitement in exploring.

She looped her brown cloth skirt over her balmoral petticoat, tied a veil round her small hat and set forth. Although the dust was flying she dared not lower her veil until she reached the environs, knowing that if she did she would be followed; or if recognized, accused of the unpardonable sin. The heavy veil in the San Francisco of that day, save when driving in aggressively respectable company, was almost an interchangeable term for assignation. It was as inconvenient for the virtuous as indiscreet for the carnal.

Madeleine reached the streets of straggling homes and those long impersonal rows depressing in their middle-class respectability, and lowered the veil over her smarting eyes. She also squared her shoulders and strode along with an independent swing that must convince the most investigating mind she was walking for exercise only.

Almost unconsciously she directed her steps toward the Cliff House Road where she had driven occasionally behind the doctor's spanking team. It was four o'clock when she entered it and the wind had fallen. The road was thronged with buggies, tandems, hacks, phaetons, and four-in-hands. Society might be out of town but the still gayer world was not. Madeleine, skirting the edge of the road to avoid disaster stared eagerly behind her veil. Here were the reckless and brilliant women of the demi-monde of whom she had heard so much, but to whom she had barely thrown a glance when driving with her husband. They were painted and dyed and kohled and their plumage would have excited the envy of birds in Paradise. San Francisco had lured these ladies "round the Horn" since the early Fifties: a different breed from the camp followers of the late Forties. Some had fallen from a high estate, others had been the mistresses of rich men in the East, or belles in the half world of New York or Paris. Never had they found life so free or pickings so easy as in San Francisco.

Madeleine knew that many of the eminent citizens she met in Society kept their mistresses and flaunted them openly. It was, in fact, almost a convention. She was not surprised to see several men who had taken her in to dinner tooling these gorgeous cyprians and looking far prouder than when they played host in the world of fashion. On one of the gayest of the coaches she saw four of the young men who were among the most devoted of her cavaliers at dances: Alexander Groome, Amos Lawton, Ogden Bascom, and "Tom" Abbott, Jr. Groome was paying his addresses to Maria Ballinger, "a fine figure of a girl" who had inherited little of her mother's beauty but all of her virtue, and Madeleine wondered if he would reform and settle down. Abbott was engaged to Marguerite McLane and looked as if he were having his last glad fling. Ogden Bascom had proposed to Guadalupe Hathaway every month for five years. It was safe to say that he would toe the mark if he won her. But he did not appear to be nursing a blighted heart at present.

Madeleine's depression left her. *That*, at least, Howard would never do. She felt full of hope and buoyancy once more, not realizing that it is easier to win back a lover than change the nature of man. When Madeleine reached the Cliff House, that shabby innocent-looking little building whose evil fame had run round the world, she stared at it fascinated. Its restaurant overhung the sea. On this side the blinds were down. It looked as if awaiting the undertaker. She pictured

Howard's horror when she told him of her close contact with vice, and anticipated with a pleasurable thrill the scolding he would give her. They had never quarrelled and it would be delightful to make up.

"Not Mrs. Talbot! No! Assuredly not!"

Involuntarily Madeleine raised her veil. She recognized the voice of "Old" Ben Travers (he was only fifty but bald and yellow), the Union Club gossip, and the one man in San Francisco she thoroughly disliked. He stood with his hat in his hand, an expression of ludicrous astonishment on his face.

"Yes, it is I," said Madeleine coolly. "And I am very much interested."

"Ah? Interested?" He glanced about. If this were an assignation either the man was late or had lost courage. But he assumed an expression of deep respect. "That I can well imagine, cloistered as you are. But, if you will permit me to say so, it is hardly prudent. Surely you know that this is a place of ill repute and that your motives, however innocent, might easily be misconstrued."

"I am alone!" said Madeleine gaily, "and my veil is up! Not a man has glanced at me, I look so tiresomely respectable in these stout walking clothes. Even you, dear Mr. Travers, whom we accuse of being quite a gossip, understand perfectly."

"Oh, yes, indeed. I do understand. And Mrs. Talbot is like Caesar's wife, but nevertheless - there is a hack. It is waiting, but I think I can bribe him to take us in. You really must not remain here another moment - and you surely do not intend to walk back - six miles?"

"No, I'll be glad to drive - but if you will engage the hack - I shouldn't think of bothering you further."

"I shall take you home," said Travers firmly. "Howard never would forgive me if I did not - that is - that is -"

Madeleine laughed merrily. "If I intend to tell him! But of course I shall tell him. Why not?"

"Well, yes, it would be best. I'll speak to the man."

The Jehu was reluctant, but a bill passed and he drove up to Madeleine. "Guess I can do it," he said, "but I'll have to drive pretty fast."

Madeleine smiled at him and he touched his hat. She had employed him more than once. "The faster the better, Thomas," she said. "I walked out and am tired."

"I saw you come striding down the road, ma'am," he said deferentially, "and I knew you got off your own beat by mistake. I think I'd have screwed up my courage and said something if Mr. Travers hadn't happened along."

Madeleine nodded carelessly and entered the hack, followed by Travers, in spite of her protests.

"I too walked out here and intended to ask some one to give me a lift home. I am the unfortunate possessor of a liver, my dear young lady, and must walk six miles a day, although I loathe walking as I loathe drinking weak whiskey and water."

Madeleine shrugged her shoulders and attempted to raise one of the curtains. The interior was as dark as a cave. But Travers exclaimed in alarm.

"No! No! Not until we get out of this. When we have reached the city, but not here. In a hack on this road -"

"Oh, very well. Then entertain me, please, as I cannot look out. You always have something interesting to tell."

"I am flattered to think you find me entertaining. I've sometimes thought you didn't like me."

"Now you know that is nonsense. I always think myself fortunate if I sit next you at dinner." Madeleine spoke in her gayest tones, but in truth she dreaded what the man might make of this innocent escapade and intended to make a friend of him if possible.

She was growing accustomed to the gloom and saw him smile fatuously. "That sends me to the seventh heaven. How often since you came have I wished that my dancing days were not over."

"I'd far rather hear you talk. Tell me some news."

"News? News? San Francisco is as flat at present as spilled champagne. Let me see? Ah! Did you ever hear of Langdon Masters?"

"No. Who is he?"

"He is Virginian like myself - a distant cousin. He fought through the war, badly wounded twice, came home to find little left of the old estate - practically nothing for him. He tried to start a newspaper in Richmond but couldn't raise the capital. He went to New York and wrote for the newspapers there; also writes a good deal for the more intellectual magazines. Thought perhaps you had come across something of his. There is just a whisper, you know, that you were rather a bas bleu before you came to us."

"Because I was born and educated in Boston? Poor Boston! I do recall reading something of Mr. Masters' in the *Atlantic* - I suppose it was - but I have forgotten what. Here, I have grown too frivolous - and happy - to care to read at all. But what have you to tell me particularly about Mr. Masters?"

"I had a letter from him this morning asking me if there was an opening here. He resents the antagonism in the North that he meets at every turn, although they are glad enough of his exceptionally brilliant work. But he knows that San Francisco is the last stronghold of the South, and also that our people are generous and enterprising. I shall write him that I can see no opening for another paper at present, but will let him know if there happens to be one on an editorial staff. That is a long journey to take on an uncertainty."

"I should think so. Heavens, how this carriage does bounce. The horses must be galloping."

"Probably." He lifted a corner of the curtain. "We shall reach the city soon at this rate. Ah!"

Madeleine, in spite of the bouncing vehicle, had managed heretofore to prop herself firmly in her corner, but a violent lurch suddenly threw her against Travers. He caught her firmly in one of his lean wiry arms. At the moment she thought nothing of it, although she disliked the contact, but when she endeavored to disengage herself, he merely jerked her more closely to his side and she felt his hot breath upon her cheek. It was the fevered breath of a man who drinks much and late and almost nauseated her.

"Come come," whispered Travers. "I know you didn't go out there to meet any one; it was just a natural impulse for a little adventure, wasn't it? And I deserve my reward for getting you home safely. Give me a kiss."

Madeleine wrenched herself free, but he laughed and caught her again, this time in both arms. "Oh, you can't get away, and I'm going to have that kiss. Yes, a dozen, by Jove. You're the prettiest thing in San Francisco, and I'll get ahead of the other men there."

His yellow distorted face - he looked like a satyr - was almost on hers. She freed herself once more with a dexterous twisting motion of her supple body, leaped to the front of the carriage and pounded on the window behind the driver.

"For God's sake! You fool! What are you doing? Do you want a scandal?"

The carriage stopped its erratic course so abruptly that he was thrown to the floor. Madeleine already had the door open. She had all the strength of youth and perfect health, and he was worn out and shaken. He was scrambling to his feet. She put her arms under his shoulders and threw him out into the road.

"Go on!" she called to the driver. And as he whipped

up the horses again, his Homeric laughter mingling with the curses of the man in the ditch, she sank back trembling and gasping. It was her first experience of the vileness of man, for the men of her day respected the women of their own class unless met half way, or, violently enamoured, given full opportunity to express their emotions.

Moreover she had made a venomous enemy.

What would Howard say? What would he do to the wretch? Horsewhip him? Would he stop to think of scandal? The road had been deserted. She knew that Travers would keep his humiliation to himself and the incidents that led up to it; but if she told her husband and he lost his head the story would come out and soon cease to bear any semblance to the truth. She wished she had some one to advise her. What *did* insulted women do?

But she could not think in this horrible carriage. It would be at least an hour before she saw Howard. She would bathe her face in cold water and try to think.

The hack stopped again and the coachman left the box.

"It's only a few blocks now, ma'am," he said, as he opened the door. "I haven't much time -"

Madeleine almost sprang out. She opened her purse. He accepted the large bill with a grin on his good-natured face.

"That's all right, Mrs. Talbot. I wouldn't have spoke of it nohow. The Doctor and me's old friends. But I'm just glad old Ben got what he deserved. The impudence of him! You - well! - Good day, ma'am."

He paused as he was climbing back to the box.

"If you don't mind my giving ye a bit of advice, Mrs. Talbot - I've seen a good bit of the world, I have - this is a hot city, all right - I just wouldn't say anything to the doctor. Trouble makes trouble. Better let it stop right here."

"Thanks, Thomas. Good-by."

And Madeleine strode down the street as if the furies pursued her.

VI

Madeleine was spared the ordeal of confession; it was six weeks before she saw her husband again. He telegraphed at six o'clock that he had a small-pox patient and could not subject her to the risk of contagion. The disease most dreaded in San Francisco had arrived some time before and the pest house outside the city limits was already crowded. The next day yellow flags appeared before several houses. Before a week passed they had multiplied all over the city. People went about with visible camphor bags suspended from their necks, and Madeleine heard the galloping death wagon at all hours of the night. Howard telegraphed frequently and sent a doctor to revaccinate her, as the virus he had administered himself had not taken. She was not to worry about him as he vaccinated himself every day. Finally he commanded her to leave town, and she made a round of visits.

She spent a fortnight at Rincona, Mrs. Abbott's place at Alta, in the San Mateo valley, and another with the Hathaways near by. Then, after a fortnight at the different "Springs" she settled down for the rest of the summer on the Ballinger ranch in the Santa Clara valley. All her hostesses had house parties, there were picnics by day and dancing or hay-rides at night. For the first time she saw the beautiful California country;

the redwood forests on the mountains, the bare brown and golden hills, the great valleys with their forests of oaks and madronas cleared here and there for orchard and vineyard; knowing that Howard was safe she gave herself to pleasure once more. After all there was a certain satisfaction in the assurance that her husband could not be with her if he would. She was not deliberately neglected and it was positive that he never entered the Club. She told no one but Sally Ballinger of her adventure, and although Travers was a favorite of her mother, this devoted friend adroitly managed that the gentleman to whom she applied many excoriating adjectives should not be invited that summer to "the ranch."

VII

Langdon Masters arrived in San Francisco during Madeleine's third winter. He did not come unheralded, for Travers bragged about him constantly and asserted that San Francisco could thank him for an editorial writer second to none in the United States of America. As a matter of fact it was on Masters' achievement alone that the editor of the *Alta California* had invited him to become a member of his staff.

Masters was also a cousin of Alexander Groome, and arrived in San Francisco as a guest at the house on Ballinger Hill, a lonely outpost in the wastes of rock and sand in the west.

There was no excitement in the female breast over his arrival for young men were abundant; but Society was prepared to welcome him not only on account of his distinguished connections but because his deliberate choice of San Francisco for his future career was a compliment they were quick to appreciate.

He came gaily to his fate filled with high hopes of owning his own newspaper before long and ranking as the leading journalist in the great little city made famous by gold and Bret Harte. He was one of many in New York; he knew that with his brilliant gifts and the immediate prominence his new position would give him the future was his to mould. No man, then or since, has brought so rare an assortment of talents to the erratic journalism of San Francisco; not even James King of William, the murdered editor of the *Evening Bulletin*. Perhaps he too would have been murdered had he remained long enough to own and edit the newspaper of his dreams, for he had a merciless irony, a fearless spirit, and an utter contempt for the prejudices of small men. But for a time at least it looked as if the history of journalism in San Francisco was to be one of California's proudest boasts.

Masters was a practical visionary, a dreamer whose dreams never confused his metallic intellect, a stylist who fascinated even the poor mind forced to express itself in colloquialisms, a man of immense erudition for his years (he was only thirty); and he was insatiably interested in the affairs of the world and in every phase of life. He was a poet by nature, and a journalist by profession because he believed the press was destined to become the greatest power in the country, and he craved not only power but the utmost opportunity for self-expression.

His character possessed as many antitheses. He was a natural lover of women and avoided them not only because he feared entanglements and enervations but because he had little respect for their brains. He was, by his Virginian inheritance, if for no simpler reason, a bon vivant, but the preoccupations and ordinary conversational subjects of men irritated him, and he cultivated their society and that of women only in so far as they were essential to his deeper understanding of life. His code was noblesse oblige and he privately damned it as a superstition foisted upon him by his ancestors. He was sentimental and ironic, passionate and indifferent, frank and subtle, proud and democratic, with a warm capacity for friendship and none whatever for intimacy, a hard worker with a strong taste for loafing - in the open country, book in hand. He prided himself upon his iron will and turned uneasily from the weeds growing among the fine flowers of his nature.

Such was Langdon Masters when he came to San Francisco and Madeleine Talbot.

VIII

He soon tired of plunging through the sand hills between the city and Ballinger Hill either on horseback or in a hack whose driver, if the hour were late, was commonly drunk; and took a suite of rooms in the Occidental Hotel. He had brought his library with him and one side of his parlor was immediately furnished with books to the ceiling. It was some time before Society saw anything of him. He had a quick reputation to make, many articles promised to Eastern periodicals and newspapers, no mind for distractions.

But his brilliant and daring editorials, not only on the pestiferous politics of San Francisco, but upon national topics, soon attracted the attention of the men; who, moreover, were fascinated by his conversation during his occasional visits to the Union Club. Several times he was cornered, royally treated to the best the cellar afforded, and upon one occasion talked for two hours, prodded merely with a question when he showed a tendency to drop into revery. But as a matter of fact he liked to talk, knowing that he could outshine other intelligent men, and a responsive palate put him in good humor with all men and inspired him with unwonted desire to please.

Husbands spoke of him enthusiastically at home and wives determined to know him. They besieged Alexina

Ballinger. Why had she not done her duty? Langdon Masters had lived in her house for weeks. Mrs. Ballinger replied that she had barely seen the man. He rarely honored them at dinner, sat up until four in the morning with her son-in-law (if she were not mistaken he and Alexander Groome were two of a feather), breakfasted at all hours, and then went directly to the city. What possible use could such a man be to Society? He had barely looked at Sally, much less the uxoriously married Maria, and might have been merely an inconsiderate boarder who had given nothing but unimpaired Virginian manners in return for so much upsetting of a household. No doubt the servants would have rebelled had he not tipped them immoderately. "Moreover," she concluded, "he is quite unlike our men, if he *is* a Southerner. And not handsome at all. His hair is black but he wears it too short, and he had no mustache, nor even sideboards. His face has deep lines and his eyes are like steel. He rarely smiles and I don't believe he ever laughed in his life."

Society, however, had made up its mind, and as the women had no particular desire to make that terrible journey to Alexina Ballinger's any oftener than was necessary, it was determined (in conclave) that Mrs. Hunt McLane should have the honor of capturing and introducing this difficult and desirable person.

Mr. McLane, who had met him at the Club, called on him formally and invited him to dinner. Hunt McLane was the greatest lawyer and one of the greatest gentlemen in San Francisco. Masters was too much a man of the world not to appreciate the compliment; moreover, he had now been in San Francisco for two months and his social instincts were stirring. He accepted the invitation and many others.

People dined early in those simple days and the hours he spent in the most natural and agreeable society he had ever entered did not interfere with his work. Sometimes he talked, at others merely listened with a pleasant sense of relaxation to the chatter of pretty women; with whom he was quite willing to flirt as long as there was no hint of the heavy vail. He thought it quite possible he should fall in love with and marry one of these vivacious pretty girls; when his future was assured in the city of his enthusiastic adoption.

He met Madeleine at all these gatherings, but it so happened that he never sat beside her and he had no taste for kettledrums or balls. He thought her very lovely to look at and wondered why so young and handsome a woman with a notoriously faithful husband should have so sad an expression. Possibly because it rather became her style of beauty.

He saw a good deal of Dr. Talbot at the Club however and asked them both to one of the little dinners in his rooms with which he paid his social debts. These dinners were very popular, for he was a connoisseur in wines, the dinner was sent from a French restaurant, and he was never more entertaining than at his own table. His guests were as carefully assorted as his wines, and if he did not know intuitively whose minds and tastes were most in harmony, or what lady did not happen to be speaking to another at the moment, he had always the delicate hints of Mrs. McLane to guide him. She was his social sponsor and vastly proud of him.

IX

Madeline went impassively to the dinner. His brilliancy had impressed her but she was indifferent to everything these days and her intellect was torpid; although when in society and under the influence of the lights and wine she could be almost as animated as ever. But the novelty of that society had worn thin long since; she continued to go out partly as a matter of routine, more perhaps because she had no other resource. She saw less of her husband than ever, for his practice as well as his masculine acquaintance grew with the city - and that was swarming over the hills of the north and out toward the sand dunes of the west. But she was resigned, and inappetent. She had even ceased to wish for children. The future stretched before her interminable and dull. A railroad had been built across the continent and she had asked permission recently of her husband to visit her parents: her mother was now an invalid and Mr. Chilton would not leave her.

But the doctor was more nearly angry than she had ever seen him. He couldn't live without her. He must always know she was "there." Moreover, she was run down, she was thin and pale, he must keep her under his eye. But if he was worried about her health he was still more worried at her apparent desire to leave him for months. Did she no longer love him? Her response was not emphatic and he went out and bought her a diamond bracelet. At least she was thankful that it had been bought for her and not sent to his wife by mistake, an experience that had happened the other day to Maria Groome. The town had rocked with laughter and Groome had made a hurried trip East on business. But Madeleine no longer found consolation in the reflection that things might be worse. The sensation of jealousy would have been a welcome relief from this spiritual and mental inertia.

She wore a dress of bright golden-green grosgrain silk trimmed with crepe leaves a shade deeper. The pointed bodice displayed her shoulders in a fashion still beloved of royal ladies, and her soft golden-brown hair was dressed in a high chignon with a long curl descending over the left side of her bust. A few still clung to the low chignon, others had adopted a fashion set by the Empress Eugenie and wore their hair in a mass of curls on the nape of the neck; but Madeleine received the latest advices from a sister-in-law who lived in New York; and as femininity dies hard she still felt a mild pleasure in introducing the latest cry in fashion. As she was the last to arrive she would have been less than woman if she had not felt a glow at the sensation she made. The color came back to her cheeks as the women surrounded her with ecstatic compliments and peered at the coiffure from all sides. The diamond bracelet was barely noticed.

"I adopt it tomorrow," said Mrs. McLane emphatically. "With my white hair I shall look more like an old marquise than ever."

One of the other women ran into Masters' bedroom where they had left their wraps and emerged in a few moments with a lifted chignon and a straggling curl. Amid exclamations and laughter two more followed suit, while the host and the other men waited patiently for their dinner. It was a lively party that finally sat down, and it was the gayest if the most momentous of Masters' little functions.

His eyes strayed toward Madeleine more than once, for her success had excited her and she had never looked lovelier. She was at the other end of the table and Mrs. McLane and Mrs. Ballinger sat beside him. She interested him for the first time and he adroitly drew her history from his mentor (not that he deluded that astute lady for an instant, but she dearly loved to gossip).

"She is going through one of those crises that all young wives must expect," she concluded. "If it isn't one thing it's another. She is still very young, and inclined to be romantic. She expected too much - of a husband, mon dieu! Of course she is lonely or thinks she is. Too bad youth never can realize that it is enough to be young. And with beauty, and means, and position, and charming frocks! She will grow philosophical - when it is too late. Meanwhile a little flirtation would not hurt her and Howard Talbot does not know the meaning of the word jealousy. Why don't you take her in hand?"

"Not my line. But it seems odd that Talbot should neglect her. She looks intelligent and she is certainly beautiful."

"Oh, Howard! He is the best of men but the worst of husbands."

Her attention was claimed by the man on her right and

at the same moment Madeleine's had evidently been drawn to the wall of books behind her. She turned, craned her neck, forgetting her partner.

Then, Masters saw a strange thing. Her eyes filled with tears and she continued to stare at the books in complete absorption until her attention was laughingly recalled.

"Now, that is odd," thought Masters. "Very odd."

She felt his keen gaze and laughed with a curious eagerness as she met his eyes. He guessed that for the first time he had interested her.

X

After dinner the men went into his den to smoke, but before his cigar was half finished he muttered something about his duty to the ladies and returned to the parlor. As he had half expected, Madeleine was standing before the books scanning their titles, and as he approached she drew her hand caressingly across a shelf devoted to the poets. The other women were gossiping at the end of the long room.

"You are fond of books!" he said abruptly.

She had not noticed his reappearance. She was startled and exclaimed passionately, "I loved them - once! But it is a long time since I have read anything but an occasional novel."

"But why? Why?"

He had powerful gray eyes and they magnetized the truth out of her.

"My husband thinks it is a woman's sole duty to look charming. He was afraid I would become a bluestocking and lose my charm and spoil my looks. I brought many books with me, but I never opened the cases and finally gave them to the Mercantile Library. I have never gone to look at them."

Gertrude Atherton

"Good heaven!" He had never felt sorrier for a woman who had asked alms of him in the street.

She was looking at him eagerly. "Perhaps - you won't mind - you will lend me - I don't think my husband would notice now - he is never at home except for breakfast and dinner -"

"Will I? For heaven's sake look upon them as your own. What will you take with you to-night?"

"Oh! Nothing! Perhaps you will send me one to-morrow?"

"One? I'll send a dozen. Let us select them now."

But at this moment the other men entered and she whispered hurriedly, "Will you select and send them? Any - any - I don't care what."

The doctor came toward them full of good wine and laughter. The books meant nothing to him. He had forgotten his wife's inexplicable taste for serious literature. He now found her quite perfect but was worried about her health. The tonics and horseback riding he had prescribed seemed to have little effect.

"I am going to take you away and send you to bed," he said jovially. "No sitting up after nine o'clock until you are yourself again, and not another ball this winter. A wife is a great responsibility, Masters. Any other woman is easier to prescribe for, but the wife of your bosom knows you so well she can fool you, as no woman who expects a bill twice a year would dare to do. Still, she's pretty good, pretty good. She's never had an attack of nerves, nor fainted yet. And as for 'blues' she doesn't know the meaning of the word. Come along, sweetheart."

Madeleine smiled half cynically, half wistfully, shook hands with her host and made him a pretty little speech, nodded to the others and went obediently to bed. The doctor, whose manners were courtly, escorted her to the door of their parlor and returned to Masters' rooms. The other women left immediately afterward, and as it was Saturday night, he and his host and Mr. McLane talked until nearly morning.

XI

By the first of June Fashion had deserted the city with its winds and fogs and dust, and Madeleine was one of the few that remained. Her husband had intended to send her to Congress Springs in the mountains of the Santa Clara Valley, but she seemed to be so much better that he willingly let her stay on, congratulating himself on the results of his treatment. She was no longer listless and was always singing at the piano when he rushed in for his dinner.

If he had been told that the cure was effected by books he would have been profoundly skeptical, and perhaps wisely so. But although Madeleine felt an almost passionate gratitude for Masters, she gave him little thought except when a new package of books arrived, or when she discussed them briefly with him in Society. He had never called.

But her mind flowered like a bit of tropical country long neglected by rain. She had thought that the very seeds of her mental desires were dead, but they sprouted during a long uninterrupted afternoon and grew so rapidly they intoxicated her. Masters had sent her in that first offering poets who had not become fashionable in Boston when she left it: Browning, Matthew Arnold and Swinburne; besides the Byron and Shelley and Keats of her girlhood. He sent her

Letters and Essays and Memoirs and Biographies that she had never read and those that she had and was glad to read again. He sent her books on art and she re-lived her days in the galleries of Europe, understanding for the first time what she had instinctively admired.

It was not only the sense of mental growth and expansion that exhilarated her, after her long drought, but the translation to a new world. She lived in the past in these lives of dead men; and as she read the biographies of great painters and musicians she shared their disappointments and forgot her own. Her emotional nature was in constant vibration, and this phenomenon was the more dangerous, as she would have argued - had she thought about it at all - that having been diverted to the intellect it must necessarily remain there.

If she had belonged to a later generation no doubt she would have taken to the pen herself, and artistic expression would - possibly - have absorbed and safe-guarded her during the remainder of her genetic years; but such a thing never occurred to her. She was too modest in the face of master work, and only queer freakish women wrote, anyhow, not ladies of her social status.

Although her thoughts rarely strayed to Masters, he hovered a sort of beneficent god in the background of her consciousness, the author of her new freedom and content; but it was only after an unusually long talk with him at a large dinner given to a party of distin-guished visitors from Europe, shortly before Society left town, that she found herself longing to discuss with him books that a week before would have been sufficient in themselves.

The opportunity did not arise however until she had been for more than a fortnight "alone" in San Francisco. She was returning from her daily brisk walk when she met him at the door of the hotel. They naturally entered and walked up the stairs together. She had immediately begun to ply him with questions, and as she unlocked the door of her parlor she invited him to enter.

He hesitated a moment. Nothing was farther from his intention than to permit his interest in this charming lonely woman to deepen; entanglements had proved fatal before to ambitious men; moreover he was almost an intimate friend of her husband. But he had no reasonable excuse, he had manifestly been sauntering when they met, and he had all the fine courtesy of the South. He followed her into the hotel parlor she had made unlike any other room in San Francisco, with the delicate French furniture and hangings her mother had bought in Paris and given her as a wedding present. A log fire was blazing. She waved her hand toward an easy chair beside the hearth, threw aside her hat and lifted her shining crushed hair with both hands, then ran over to a panelled chest which the doctor had conceded to be handsome, but quite useless as it was not even lined with cedar.

"I keep them in here," she exclaimed as gleefully as a naughty child; and he had the uneasy sense of sharing a secret with her that isolated them on a little oasis of their own in this lawless waste of San Francisco.

She had opened the chest and was rummaging.

"What shall it be first? How I have longed to talk with you about a dozen. On the whole I think I'd rather you'd read a poem to me. Do you mind? I know you are not lazy - oh, no! - and I am sure you read delightfully."

"I don't mind in the least," he said gallantly. (At all events he was in for it.) "And I rather like the sound of my own voice. What shall it be?"

And, alas, she chose "The Statue and the Bust."

XII

He was disconcerted, but his sense of humor come to his rescue, and although he read that passionate poem with its ominous warning to hesitant lovers, with the proper emphasis and as much feeling as he dared, he managed to make it a wholly impersonal performance. When he finished he dropped the book and glanced over at his companion. She was sitting forward with a rapt expression, her cheeks flushed, her breath coming unevenly. But there was neither challenge nor self-consciousness in her eyes. The sparkle had left them, but it was their innocence, not their melting, that stirred him profoundly. With her palimpsest mind she was a poet for the moment, not a woman.

Her manners never left her and she paid him a conventional little compliment on his reading, then asked him if he believed that people who could love like that had ever lived, or if such dramas were the peculiar prerogative of the divinely gifted imagination.

He replied drily that a good many people in their own time loved recklessly and even more disastrously, and then asked her irresistibly (for he was a man if a wary one) if she had never loved herself.

"Oh, of course," she replied simply. "I love my husband. But domestic love - how different!"

"But have you never - domestic love does not always - well -"

She shrugged her shoulders and replied with the same disconcerting simplicity, "Oh, when you are married you are married. And now that your books have made me so happy I never find fault with Howard any more. I know that he cannot be changed and he loves me devotedly in his fashion. Mrs. McLane is always preaching philosophy and your books have shown me the way."

"And do you imagine that books will always fill your life? After the novelty has worn off?"

"Oh, that could never be! Even if you went away and took your books with you I should get others. I am quite emancipated now."

"This is the first time I ever heard a young and beautiful woman declare that books were an adequate substitute for life. And one sort of emancipation is very likely to lead to another."

She drew herself up and all her Puritan forefathers looked from her candid eyes. "If you mean that I would do the things that a few of our women do - not many (she was one of the loyal guardians of her anxious little circle) - if you think - but of course you do not. That is so completely out of the question that I have never given it consideration. If my husband should die - and I should feel terribly if he did - but if he should, while I was still young, I might, of course, love another man whose tastes were exactly like my own. But I'd never betray Howard - nor myself - even in thought."

The words and all they implied might have been an irresistible challenge to another man. But to Masters, whose career was inexorably mapped out, - he was determined that his own fame and that of California should be synchronous - and who fled at the first hint of seduction in a woman's eyes, they came as a pleasurable reassurance. After all, mental companionship with a woman was unique, and it was quite in keeping that he should find it in this unique city of his adoption. Moreover, it would be a very welcome recreation in his energetic life. If propinquity began to sprout its deadly fruit he fancied that she would close the episode abruptly. He was positive that he should, if for no other reason than because her husband was his friend. He might elope with the wife of a friend if he lost his head, but he would never dishonor himself in the secret intrigue. And he had not the least intention of leaving San Francisco. For the time being they were safe. It was like picking wild flowers in the field after a day's hot work.

"Now," she said serenely, "read me 'Pippa Passes.'"

XIII

Nevertheless, he stayed away from her for a week. At the end of that time he received a peremptory little note bidding him call and expound Newman's "Apologia" to her. She could not understand it and she must.

He smiled at the pretty imperiousness of the note so like herself; for her circle had spoiled her, and whatever her husband's idiosyncrasies she was certainly his petted darling.

He went, of course. And before long he was spending every afternoon in the charming room so like a French salon of the Eighteenth Century that the raucous sounds of San Francisco beyond the closed and curtained windows beat upon it faintly like the distant traffic of a great city.

Masters had asked himself humorously, Why not? and succumbed. There was no other place to go except the Club, and Mrs. Talbot was an infinitely more interesting companion than men who discussed little besides their business, professional, or demi-monde engrossments. It was a complete relaxation from his own driving work. He was writing the entire editorial page of his newspaper, the demand for his articles from Eastern magazines and weekly journals was

Gertrude Atherton

incessant; which not only contributed to his pride and income, but to the glory of California. He was making her known for something besides gold, gamblers, and Sierra pines.

But above all he was instructing and expanding a feminine but really fine mind. She sat at his feet and there was no doubt in that mind, both naive and gifted, that his was the most remarkable intellect in the world and that from no book ever written could she learn as much. He would have been more than mortal had he renounced his pedestal and he was far too humane for the cruelty of depriving her of the stimulating happiness he had brought into her lonely life. There was no one, man or woman, to take his place.

Nor was there any one to criticize. The world was out of town. They lived in the same hotel, and he rarely met any one in their common corridor. At first she mentioned his visits casually to her husband, and Howard grunted approvingly. Several times he took Masters snipe shooting in the marshes near Ravenswood, but he accepted his friend's attitude to his wife too much as a matter of course even to mention it. To him, a far better judge of men than of women, Langdon Masters was ambition epitomized, and if he wondered why such a man wasted time in any woman's salon, he concluded it was because, like men of any calling but his own (who saw far too much of women and their infernal ailments) he enjoyed a chat now and then with as charming a woman of the world as Madeleine. If anyone had suggested that Langdon Masters enjoyed Madeleine's intellect he would have told it about town as the joke of the season.

Madeleine indulged in no introspection. She had

suffered too much in the past not to quaff eagerly of the goblet when it was full and ask for nothing more. If she paused to realize how dependent she had become on the constant society of Langdon Masters and that literature was now no more than the background of life, she would have shrugged her shoulders gaily and admitted that she was having a mental flirtation, and that, at least, was as original as became them both. They were safe. The code protected them. He was her husband's friend and they were married. What was, was.

But in truth she never went so far as to admit that Masters and the books she loved were not one and inseparable. She could not imagine herself talking with him for long on any other subject, save, perhaps, the politics of the nation - which, in truth, rather bored her. As for small talk she would as readily have thought of inflicting the Almighty in her prayers.

Nor was it often they drifted into personalities or the human problems. One day, however, he did ask her tentatively if she did not think that divorce was justifiable in certain circumstances.

She merely stared at him in horror.

"Well, there is your erstwhile friend, Sibyl Geary. She fell in love with another man, her husband was a sot, she got her divorce without legal opposition, and married Forbes - finest kind of fellow."

"Divorce is against the canons of Church and Society. No woman should break her solemn vows, no matter what her provocation. Look at Maria Groome. Do you think she would divorce Alexander? She has provocation enough."

"You are both High Church, but all women are not. Mrs. Geary is a mere Presbyterian. And at least she is as happy as she was wretched before."

"No woman can be happy who has lost the respect of Society."

"I thought you were bored with Society."

"Yes, but it is mine to have. Being bored is quite different from being cast out like a pariah."

"Oh! And you think love a poor substitute?"

"Love, of course, is the most wonderful thing in the world. (She might be talking of maternal or filial love, thought Masters.) But it must have the sanction of one's principles, one's creed and one's traditions. Otherwise, it weighs nothing in the balance."

"You are a delectable little Puritan," said Masters with a laugh that was not wholly mirthful. "I shall now read you Tennyson's 'Maud,' as you approve of sentiment, at least. Tennyson will never cause the downfall of any woman, but if you ever see lightning on the horizon don't read 'The Statue and the Bust' with the battery therof."

XIV

When people returned to town they were astonished at the change in Madeleine Talbot, especially after a summer in the city that would have "torn their own nerves out by the roots." More than one had wondered anxiously if she were going into the decline so common in those days. They had known the cause of the broken spring, but none save the incurably sanguine opined that Howard Talbot had mended it. But mended it was and her eyes had never sparkled so gaily, nor her laugh rung so lightly since her first winter among them. Mrs. McLane suggested charitably that her tedium vitae had run its course and she was become a philosopher.

But Madeleine *reviva* did not suggest the philosopher to the most charitable eye (not even to Mrs. McLane's), particularly as there was a "something" about her - was it repressed excitement? - which had been quite absent from her old self, however vivacious.

It was Mrs. Abbott, a lady of unquenchable virtue, whose tongue was more feared than that of any woman in San Francisco, who first verbalized what every friend of Madeleine's secretly wondered: Was there a man in the case? Many loyally cried, Impossible. Madeleine was above suspicion. Above suspicion, yes. No one would accuse her of a liaison. But who was she or any other neglected young wife to be above falling in love if some fascinating creature laid siege? Love dammed up was apt to spring a leak in time, even if it did not overflow, and - well, it was known that water sought its level, even if it could not run uphill. Mrs. Abbott had lived for twenty years in San Francisco, and in New Orleans for thirty years before that, and she had seen a good many women in love in her time. This climate made a plaything of virtue. "Virtue - you said? - Precisely. She's *not there* or we'd see the signs of moral struggle, horror, in fact; for she's not one to succumb easily. But mark my words, *she's on the way*."

That point settled, and it was vastly interesting to believe it (Madeleine Talbot, of all people!), who was the man? Duty to mundane affairs had kept many of the liveliest blades and prowling husbands in town all summer; but Madeleine had known them all for three years or more. Besides, So and So was engaged to So and So, and So and So quite reprehensibly interested in Mrs. So and So.

The young gentlemen were discreetly sounded, but their lack of anything deeper than friendly interest in the "loveliest of her sex" was manifest. Husbands were ordered to retail the gossip of the Club, but exploded with fury when tactful pumping forced up the name of Madeleine Talbot. They were harridans, harpies, old-wives, infernal scandalmongers. If there was one completely blameless woman in San Francisco it was Howard Talbot's wife.

No one thought of Langdon Masters.

He appeared more rarely at dinners, and had never

ventured in public with Madeleine even during the summer. When his acute news sense divined they were gossiping and speculating about her he took alarm and considered the wisdom of discontinuing his afternoon visits. But they had become as much a part of his life as his daily bread. Moreover, he could not withdraw without giving the reason, and it was a more intimate subject than he cared to discuss with her. Whether he was in love with her or not was a question he deliberately refused to face. If the present were destroyed there was no future to take its place, and he purposed to live in his Fool's Paradise as long as he could. It was an excellent substitute for tragedy.

But Society soon began to notice that she no longer honored kettledrums or the more formal afternoon receptions with her presence, and her calls were few and late. When attentive friends called on her she was "out." The clerk at the desk had been asked to protect her, as she "must rest in the afternoon." He suspected nothing and her word was his law.

When quizzed, Madeleine replied laughingly that she could keep her restored health only by curtailing her social activities; but she blushed, for lying came hardly. As calling was a serious business in San Francisco, she compromised by the ancient clearing-house device of an occasional large "At Home," besides her usual dinners and luncheons. When Masters was a dinner guest he paid her only the polite attentions due a hostess and flirted elaborately with the prettiest of the women. Madeleine, who was unconscious of the gossip, was sometimes a little hurt, and when he avoided her at other functions and was far too attentive to Sally Ballinger, or Annette McLane, a beautiful girl just out, she had an odd palpitation and wondered what ailed her. Jealous? Well, perhaps. Friends of the same sex were often jealous. Had not Sally been jealous at one time of poor Sibyl Geary? And Masters was the most complete friend a woman ever had. She thought sadly that perhaps he had enough of her in the afternoon and welcomed a change. Well, that was natural enough. She found herself enjoying the society of other bright men at dinners, now that life was fair again.

Nevertheless, she experienced a sensation of fright now and again, and not because she feared to lose him.

XV

There is nothing so carking as the pangs of unsatisfied curiosity. They may not cause the acute distress of love and hate, but no tooth ever ached more incessantly nor more insistently demanded relief. That doughty warrior, Mrs. Abbott, in her own homely language determined to take the bull by the horns. She sailed into the Occidental Hotel one afternoon and up the stairs without pausing at the desk. The clerk gave her a cursory glance. Mrs. Abbott went where she listed, and, moreover, was obviously expected.

When she reached the Talbot parlor she halted a moment, and then knocked loudly. Madeleine, who often received parcels, innocently invited entrance. Mrs. Abbott promptly accepted the invitation and walked in upon Masters and his hostess seated before the fire. The former had a book in his hand, and, judging from the murmur that had penetrated her applied ear before announcing herself, had been reading aloud. ("As cozy as two bugs in a rug," she told her friends afterward.)

"Oh, Mrs. Abbott! How kind of you!" Madeleine was annoyed to find herself blushing, but she kept her head and entered into no explanation. Masters, with his most politely aloof air, handed the smiling guest to the sofa, and as she immediately announced that the room was too warm for her, Madeleine removed her dolman. Mrs. Abbott as ever was clad in righteous black satin trimmed with bugles and fringe, and a small flat bonnet whose strings indifferently supported her chins. She fixed her sharp small eyes immediately on Madeleine's beautiful house gown of nile green camel's hair, made with her usual sweeping lines and without trimming of any sort.

"Charming - charming - and so becoming with that lovely color you have. New York, I suppose -"

"Oh, no, a seamstress made it. You must let me get you cake and a glass of wine." The unwilling hostess crossed over to the hospitable cupboard and Mrs. Abbott amiably accepted a glass of port, the while her eyes could hardly tear themselves from the books on the table by the fire. There were at least a dozen of them and her astute old mind leapt straight at the truth.

"I thought you had given all your books to the Mercantile Library," she remarked wonderingly. "We all thought it so hard on you, but Howard is set in his ways, poor old thing. He was much too old for you anyhow. I always said so. But I see he has relented. Have you been patronizing C. Beach? Nice little book store. I go there myself at Christmas time - get a set in nice bindings for one of the children every year."

"Oh, these are borrowed," said Madeleine lightly. "Mr. Masters has been kind enough to lend them to me."

"Oh - h - h, naughty puss! What would Howard say if he found you out?"

Masters, who stood on the hearth rug, looked down at

her with an expression, which, she afterward confessed, sent shivers up her spine. "Talbot is a great friend of mine," he said with deliberate emphasis, "and not likely to object to his wife's sharing my library."

"Don't be too sure. The whole town knows that Howard detests bluestockings and would rather his wife had a good honest flirtation than stuffed her brains.... Pretty little head." She tweaked Madeleine's scarlet ear. "Mustn't put too much in it."

"I'm afraid it doesn't hold much," said Madeleine smiling; and fancied she heard a bell in her depths toll: "It's going to end! It's going to end!" And for the first time in her life she felt like fainting.

She went hurriedly over to the cupboard and poured herself out a glass of port wine. "I had almost forgotten my tonic," she said. "It has made me quite well again."

"Your improvement is nothing short of miraculous," said the old lady drily. "It is the talk of the town. But you are ungrateful if you don't give all those interesting books some of the credit. I hope Howard is properly grateful to Mr. Masters.... By the way, my young friend, the men complain that you are never seen at the Club during the afternoon any more. That is ungrateful, if you like! - for they all think you are the brightest man out here, and would rather hear you talk than eat - or drink, which is more to the point. Now, I must go, dear. I won't intrude any longer. It has been delightful, meeting two such clever people at once. You are coming to my 'At Home' tomorrow. I won't take no for an answer."

There was a warning note in her voice. Her pointed

remarks had not been inspired by sheer felinity. It was her purpose to let Madeleine know that she was in danger of scandal or worse, and that the sooner she scrambled back to terra firma the better. Of course she could not refrain from an immediate round of calls upon impatient friends, but she salved her conscience by asserting roundly (and with entire honesty) that there was nothing in it as yet. She had seen too much of the world to be deceived on *that* point.

XVI

After Masters had assisted Mrs. Abbott's large bulk into her barouche, resisting the impulse to pitch it in headfirst, he walked slowly up the stairs. He was seething with fury, and he was also aghast. The woman had unquestionably precipitated the crisis he had hoped to avoid. To use her favorite expression, the fat was in the fire; and she would see to it that it was maintained at sizzling point. He ground his teeth as he thought of the inferences, the innuendos, the expectations, the constant linking of his name with Madeleine's. Madeleine!

It was true, of course, that the gossip might stop short of scandal if she entered the afternoon treadmill once more and showed herself so constantly that the most malignant must admit that she had no time for dalliance; it was well known that he spent the morning and late afternoon hours at the office.

But that would mean that he must give her up. She was the last woman to consent to stolen meetings, even were he to suggest them, for the raison d'etre of their companionship would be gone. And that phase could end in but one way.

What a dreamer he had been, he, a man of the world, to imagine that such an idyll could last. Perhaps four perfect months were as much as a man had any right to ask of life. Nevertheless, he experienced not the slightest symptom of resignation. He felt reckless enough to throw his future to the winds, kidnap Madeleine, and take the next boat to South America. But his unclouded mind drove inexorably to the end: her conscience and unremitting sense of disgrace would work the complete unhappiness of both. Divorce was equally out of the question.

As he approached her door he felt a strong inclination to pass it and defer the inevitable interview until the morrow. He must step warily with her as with the world, and he needed all his self-control. If he lost his head and told her that he loved her he would not save a crumb from his feast. Moreover, there was the possibility of revealing her to herself if she loved him, and that would mean utter misery for her.

Did she? He walked hastily past her door. His coolly reasoning brain felt suddenly full of hot vapors.

Then he cursed himself for a coward and turned back. She would feel herself deserted in her most trying hour, for she needed a reassuring friend at this moment if never before. He had rarely failed to keep his head when he chose and he would keep it now.

But when he entered the room his self-command was put to a severe test. She was huddled in a chair crying, and although he scoffed at woman's tears as roundly as Dr. Talbot, they never failed to rain on the softest spot in his nature. But he walked directly to the hearth rug and lit a cigarette.

"I hope you are not letting that old cat worry you." He

managed to infuse his tones with an amiable contempt.

But Madeleine only cried the harder.

"Come, come. Of course you are bruised, you are such a sensitive little plant, but you know what women are, and more especially that old woman. But even she cannot find much to gossip about in the fact that you were receiving an afternoon caller."

"It - is - is - n't - only that!"

"What, then?"

"I - I'll be back in a moment."

She ran into her bedroom, and Masters took a batch of proofs from his pocket and deliberately read them during the ten minutes of her absence. When she returned she had bathed her eyes, and looked quite composed. In truth she had taken sal volatile, and if despair was still in her soul her nerves no longer jangled.

He rose to hand her a chair, but she shook her head and walked over to the window, then returned and stood by the table, leaning on it as if to steady herself.

"Shall I get you a glass of port wine?"

"No; more than one goes to my head."

He threw the proofs on the table and retreated to the hearth-rug.

"I suppose this means that you must not come here

any more?"

"Does it? Are you going to turn me adrift to bore myself at the Club?"

"Oh, men have so many resources! And it is you who have given all. I had nothing to give you."

"You forget, my dear Mrs. Talbot, that man is never so flattered as when some woman thinks him an oracle. Besides, although yours is the best mind in any pretty woman's head I know of - in any woman's head for that matter - you still have much to learn, and I should feel very jealous if you learned it elsewhere."

"Oh, I could learn from books, I suppose. There are many more in the world than I shall ever be able to read. But - well, I had a friend for the first time - the kind of friend I wanted."

"You are in no danger of losing him. I haven't the least intention of giving you up. Real friendships are too rare, especially those founded on mental sympathy, and a man's life is barren indeed when his friends are only men."

"Have you had any woman friends before?" Her eyelids were lowered but she shot him a swift glance.

"Well - no - to be honest, I cannot say I have. Flirtations and all that, yes. During the last eight years, between the war and earning my bread, I've had little time. Everything went, of course. I wrote for a while for a Richmond paper and then went to New York. That was hard sledding for a time and Southerners are not welcome in New York Society. If I bore you with my personal affairs it is merely to give you a glimpse of a rather arid life, and, perhaps, some idea of how pleasant and profitable I have found our friendship."

She drooped her head. He ground his teeth and lit another cigarette. His hand trembled but his tones were even and formal.

"I shall go to Mrs. Abbott's tomorrow."

"Quite right. And if a man strays in flirt with him - if you know how."

"There are four other At Homes and kettledrums this week and I shall go to those also. I don't know that I mind silly gossip, but it would not be fair to Howard. I shouldn't like to put him in the position of some men in this town; although they seem to console themselves! But Howard is not like that."

"Not he. The best fellow in the world. I think your program admirable." He saw that he was trying her too far and added hastily: "It would be rather amusing to circumvent them, and it certainly would not amuse me to lose your charming companionship. I have fallen into the habit of imposing myself upon you from three until five or half-past. Perhaps you will admit me shortly after lunch and let me hang round until you are ready to go out?"

She looked up with faintly sparkling eyes; then her face fell.

"There are so many luncheons."

"But surely not every day. You could refuse the

informal affairs on the plea of a previous engagement, and give me the list of the inevitable ones the first of the week. And at least you are free from impertinent intrusion before three o'clock."

"Yes, I'll do that! I will! It will be better than nothing."

"Oh, a long sight better. And nothing can alter the procession of the seasons. Summer will arrive again in due course, and if your friends are not far more interested in something else by that time it is hardly likely that even Mrs. Abbott will sacrifice the comforts of Alta to spy on any one."

"Not she! She has asthma in San Francisco in summer." Madeleine spoke gaily, but she avoided his eyes. Whether he was maintaining a pose or not she could only guess, but she had one of her own to keep up.

"You must have thought me very silly to cry - but - these people have all been quite angelic to me before, and Mrs. Abbott descended upon me like the Day of Judgment."

"I should think she did, the old she-devil, and if you hadn't cried you wouldn't have been a true woman! But we have a good half hour left. I'd like to read you -"

At this moment Dr. Talbot's loud voice was heard in the hall.

"All right. See you later. Sorry -"

XVII

Madeline caught at the edge of the table. Had he met Mrs. Abbott? But even in this moment of consternation she avoided a glance of too intimate understanding with Masters. She was reassured immediately, however. The Doctor burst into the room and exclaimed jovially:

"You here? What luck. Thought you would be at some infernal At Home or other. Just got a call to San Jose - consultation - must take the next train. Come, help me pack. Hello, Masters. If I'd had time I'd have looked you up. Got some news for you. Wait a moment."

He disappeared into his bedroom and Madeleine followed. He had not noticed the books and Masters' first impulse was to gather them up and replace them in the chest. But he sat down to his proofs instead. The Doctor returned in a few moments.

"Madeleine will finish. She's a wonder at packing. Hello! What's this?" He had caught sight of the books.

"Some of mine. Mrs. Talbot expressed a wish -"

"Why in thunder don't you call her Madeleine? You're as much her friend as mine.... Well, I don't mind as much as I did, for I find women are all reading more than they used to, and I'm bound to say they don't have the blues while a good novel lasts. Ouida's a pretty good dose and lasts about a week. But don't give her too much serious stuff. It will only addle her brains."

"Oh, she has very good brains. Mrs. Abbott was here just now, and although she is not what I should call literary - or too literate - she seemed to think your wife was just the sort of woman who should read."

"Mrs. Abbott's a damned old nuisance. You must have been overjoyed at the interruption. But if Madeleine has to put on pincenez -"

"Oh, never fear!" Madeleine was smiling radiantly as she entered. Her volatile spirits were soaring. "My eyes are the strongest part of me. What did you have to tell Mr. Masters?" "Jove! I'd almost forgotten, and it's great news, too. What would you say, Masters, to editing a paper of your own?"

"What?"

"There's a conspiracy abroad - I won't deny I had a hand in it - no light under the bushel for me - to raise the necessary capital and have a really first-class newspaper in this town. San Francisco deserves the best, and if we've had nothing but rags, so far - barring poor James King of William's *Bulletin* - it's because we've never had a man before big enough to edit a great one."

"I have no words! It is almost too good to be true!"

Madeleine watched him curiously. His voice was trembling and his eyes were flashing. He was tall but had drawn himself up in his excitement and seemed quite an inch taller. He looked about to wave a sword and lead a charge. Establishing a newspaper meant a hard fight and he was eager for the fray.

She had had but few opportunities to study him in detail unobserved. She had never thought him handsome, for he was clean shaven, with deep vertical lines, and he wore his black hair very short. Her preference was for fair men with drooping moustaches and locks sweeping the collar; although her admiration for this somewhat standardized type had so far been wholly impersonal. Even the doctor clipped his moustache as it interfered with his soup, and his rusty brown hair was straight, although of the orthodox length. But she had not married Howard for his looks!

She noted the hard line of jaw and sharp incisive profile. His face had power as well as intellect, yet there was a hint of weakness somewhere. Possibly the lips of his well-cut mouth were a trifle too firmly set to be unselfconscious. And his broad forehead lacked serenity. There was a furrow between the eyes.

It was with the eyes she was most familiar. They were gray, brilliant, piercing, wide apart and deeply set. She had noted more than once something alert, watchful, in their expression, as if they were the guardians of the intellect above and defied the weakness the lower part of his face barely hinted to clash for a moment with his ambitions.

She heard little of his rapid fire of questions and Howard's answers; but when the doctor had pulled out his watch, kissed her hurriedly, snatched his bag and dashed from the room, Masters took her hands in his,

his eyes glowing.

"Did you hear?" he cried. "Did you hear? I am to have my own newspaper. My dream has come true! A hundred thousand dollars are promised. I shall have as good a news service as any in New York."

Madeleine withdrew her hands but smiled brightly and made him a pretty speech of congratulation. She knew little of newspapers and cared less, but there must be something extraordinary about owning one to excite a man like Langdon Masters. She had never seen him excited before.

"Won't it mean a great deal harder work?"

"Oh, work! I thrive on work. I've never had enough. Come and sit down. Let me talk to you. Let me be egotistical and talk about myself. Let me tell you all my pent-up ambitions and hopes and desires - you wonderful little Egeria!"

And he poured himself out to her as he had never unbosomed himself before. He stayed on to dinner - she had no engagement - and left her only for the office. He had evidently forgotten the earlier episode, and he swept it from her own mind. That mind, subtle, feminine, yielding, melted into his. She shared those ambitions and hopes and desires. His brilliant and useful future was as real and imperative to her as to himself. It was a new, a wonderful, a thrilling experience. When she went to bed, smiling and happy, she slammed a little door in her mind and shot the bolt. A terrible fear had shaken her three hours before, but she refused to recall it. Once more the present sufficed.

XVIII

Madeleine went to Mrs. Abbott's reception, but there was nothing conciliatory nor apologetic in her mien. She had intended to be merely natural, but when she met that battery of eyes, amused, mocking, sympathetic, encouraging, and realized that Mrs. Abbott's tongue had been wagging, she was filled with an anger and resentment that expressed itself in a cold pride of bearing and a militant sparkle of the eye. She was gracious and aloof and Mrs. McLane approved her audibly.

"Exactly as I should feel and look myself," she said to Mrs. Ballinger and Guadalupe Hathaway. "She's a royal creature and she has moved in the great world. No wonder she resents the petty gossip of this village."

"Well, I'll acquit her," said Mrs. Ballinger tartly. "A more cold-blooded and unattractive man I've never met."

"Langdon Masters is by no means unattractive," announced Miss Hathaway out of her ten years' experience as a belle and an unconscionable flirt. "I have sat in the conservatory with him several times. It may be that Mrs. Abbott stepped in before it was too late. And it may be that she did not."

"Oh, call no woman virtuous until she is dead," said Mrs. McLane lightly. "But I won't hear another insinuation against Madeleine Talbot."

Mrs. Abbott kissed the singed brand it had been her mission to snatch in the nick of time and detained her in conversation with unusual empressement. Madeleine responded with an excessive politeness, and Mrs. Abbott learned for the first time that sweet brown eyes could glitter as coldly as her own protuberant orbs when pronouncing judgment.

Madeleine remained for two hours, bored and disgusted, the more as Masters' name was ostentatiously avoided. Even Sally Ballinger, who kissed her warmly, told her that she looked as if she hadn't a care in the world and that it was because she had too much sense to bother about men!

She had never been treated with more friendly intimacy, and if she went home with a headache it was at least a satisfaction to know that her proud position was still scandal-proof.

She wisely modified her first program and drifted back into afternoon society by degrees; a plan of defensive campaign highly approved by Mrs. McLane, who detested lack of finesse. The winter was an unsatisfactory one for Madeleine altogether. Society would not have bored her so much perhaps if that secret enchanting background had remained intact. But her intercourse with Masters was necessarily sporadic. Her conscience had never troubled her for receiving his visits, for her husband not only had expressed his approval, but had always urged her to amuse herself with men. But she felt like an intriguante when she discussed her engagement lists with Masters, and she knew that he liked it as little. His visits were now a matter for "sandwiching," to be schemed and planned for, and she dared not ask herself whether the persistent sense of fear that haunted her was that they both must betray self-consciousness in time, or that the more difficult order would bore him: their earlier intimacy had coincided with his hours of leisure. After all, he was not her lover, to delight in intrigue; and in time, it might be, he would not think the game worth the candle. She dreaded that revived gossip might drive him from the hotel, and that would be the miserable beginning of an unthinkable end.

There were other interruptions. He paid a flying visit to Richmond to visit the death-bed of his mother, and he took a trip to the Sandwich Islands to recover from a severe cold on the chest. Moreover, his former placidity had left him, for one thing and another delayed the financing of his newspaper. One of its founders was temporarily embarrassed for ready money, another awaited an opportune moment to realize on some valuable stock. There was no doubt that the entire amount would be forthcoming in time, but meanwhile he fumed, and expressed himself freely to Madeleine. That he might have a more poisonous source of irritation did not occur to her.

Fortunately she did not suspect that gossip was still rife. Madeleine might have a subtle mind but she had a candid personality. It was quite patent to sharp eyes that she was unhappy once more, although this time her health was unaffected. And Society was quite aware that she still saw Langdon Masters, in spite of her perfunctory appearances; for suspicion once roused develops antennae that traverse space without effort and return with accumulated minute stores of evidence. Masters had been seen entering or leaving the Talbot parlor by luncheon guests in the hotel. Old Ben Travers, who had chosen to ignore his astonishing and humiliating experience and always treated Madeleine with exaggerated deference, called one afternoon on her (in company with Mrs. Ballinger) and observed cigarette ends in the ash tray. Talbot smoked only cigars. Masters was one of the few men in San Francisco who smoked cigarettes and there was no mistaking his imported brand. Mr. Travers paid an immediate round of visits, and called again a fortnight later, this time protected by Mrs. Abbott. There were several books on the table which he happened to know Masters had received within the week.

When the new wave reached Mrs. McLane she announced angrily that all the gossip in San Francisco originated in the Union Club, and refused to listen to details. But she was anxious, nevertheless, for she knew that Madeleine, whether she recognized the fact or not, was in love with Langdon Masters, and she more than suspected that he was with her. He went little into society, even before his mother's death, pleading press of work, but Mr. McLane often brought him home quietly to dinner and she saw more of him than any one did but Madeleine. Men had gone mad over her in her own time and she knew the stamp of baffled passions.

It was on New Year's Day, during Masters' absence in Richmond, that an incident occurred which turned Society's attention, diverted for the moment by an open divorce scandal, to Madeleine Talbot once more.

XIX

New Year's Day in San Francisco was one of pomp and triumphs, and much secret heart-burning. Every woman who had a house threw it open and the many that lived in hotels were equally hospitable. There was a constant procession of family barouches, livery stable buggies and hacks. The "whips" drove their mud-bespattered traps with as grand an air as if on the Cliff House Road in fine weather; and while none was ignored whose entertaining was lavish, those who could count only on admiration and friendship compared notes eagerly during the following week.

But young men in those days were more gallant or less snobbish than in these, and few pretty girls, however slenderly dowered, were forgotten by their waltzing partners. The older men went only to the great houses, and frankly for eggnog. Mrs. Abbott's was famous and so was Mrs. McLane's. Ladies who lived out of town the year round, that their husbands might "sleep in the country!" received with their more fortunate friends.

It had been Madeleine's intention to have her own reception at the hotel as usual, but when Mrs. McLane craved her assistance - Marguerite was receiving with Mrs. Abbott, now her mother-in-law - she consented willingly, as it would reduce her effort to entertain progressively illuminated men to the minimum. She felt disinclined to effort of any sort.

Mrs. McLane, after her daughter's marriage, had tired of the large house on Rincon Hill and the exorbitant wages of its staff of servants, and returned to her old home in South Park, furnishing her parlors with a red satin damask, which also covered the walls. She had made a trip to Paris meanwhile and brought back much light and graceful French furniture. The long double room was an admirable setting for her stately little figure in its trailing gown of wine-colored velvet trimmed with mellowed point lace (it had been privately dipped in coffee) and her white high-piled hair. There was no watchful anxiety in Mrs. McLane's lofty mien. She knew that the best, old and young, would come to her New Year's Day reception as a matter of course.

Mrs. Ballinger had also gratefully accepted Mrs. McLane's invitation, for Sally had recently married Harold Abbott and was receiving on Rincon Hill, and Maria was in modest retirement. She wore a long gown of silver gray poplin as shining as her silver hair; and as she was nearly a foot taller than her hostess, the two ladies stood at opposite ends of the mantelpiece in the front parlor with Annette McLane and two young friends between.

The reception was at its height at four o'clock. The rooms were crowded, and the equipages of the guests packed not only South Park but Third Street a block north and south.

Madeleine sat at the end of the long double room behind a table and served the eggnog. The men hovered about her, not, as commonly, in unqualified admiration, or passed on the goblets, slices of the monumental cakes, and Peter Job's famous cream pie.

She had taken a glass at once and raised her spirits to the necessary pitch; but its effect wore off in time and her hand began to tremble slightly as she ladled out the eggnog. She had not heard from Masters since he left and her days were as vacant as visible space. She had felt nervous and depressed since morning and would have spent the day in bed had she dared.

Mr. McLane, Mr. Abbott, Colonel "Jack" Belmont, Alexander Groome, Mr. Ballinger, Amos Lawton and several others were chatting with her when Ben Travers sauntered up to demand his potion. He had already paid several visits, and although he carried his liquor well, it was patent to the eyes of his friends he was in that particular stage of inebriation that swamped his meagre stock of good nature and the superficial cleverness which made him an agreeable companion, and set free all the maliciousness of a mind contracted with years and disappointments: he had never made "his pile" and it was current history that he had been refused by every belle of his youth.

He made Madeleine a courtly bow as he took the goblet from her hands, not forgetting to pay her a well-turned compliment on those hands, not the least of her physical perfections. Then he balanced himself on the edge of the table with a manifest intention of joining in the conversation. Madeleine felt an odd sense of terror, although she knew nothing of his discoveries and communications; there was a curious hard stare in his bleared eyes and it seemed to impale her.

He began amiably enough. "Best looking frocks in this

house I've seen today. At least five from Paris. Mrs. McLane brought back four of them besides her own. Seen some awful old duds today. 'Lupie Hathaway had on an old black silk with a gaping placket and three buttons off in front. Some of the other things were new enough, but the dressmakers in this town need waking up. Of course yours came from New York, Mrs. Talbot. Charming, simply charming."

Madeleine wore a gown of amber-colored silk with a bertha of fine lace and mousseline de soie, exposing her beautiful shoulders. The color seemed reflected in her eyes and the bright waving masses of her hair.

"Madame Deforme made it," she said triumphantly. "Now don't criticize our dressmakers again."

"Never criticize anybody but can't help noticing things. Got the observing eye. Nothing escapes it. How are you off for books now that Masters has deserted us?"

Madeleine turned cold, for the inference was unmistakable, and she saw Mr. McLane scowl at him ferociously, But she replied smilingly that there was always the Mercantile Library.

"Never have anything new there, and even C. Beach hasn't had a new French novel for six months. If Masters were one of those considerate men, now, he'd have left you the key of his rooms. Nothing compromising in that. But it would be no wonder if he forgot it, for I hear it wasn't his mother's illness that took him to Richmond, but Betty Thornton who's still a reigning toast. Old flame and they say she's come round. Had a letter from my sister."

Madeleine, who was lifting a goblet, let it fall with a crash. She had turned white and was trembling, but she lifted another with an immediate return of self-control, and said, "How awkward of me! But I have had a headache for three days and the gas makes the room so warm."

And then she fainted.

Mr. McLane, who was more impulsive than tactful, took Travers by the arm and pushed him through the crowd surging toward the table, and out of the front door, almost flinging him down the front steps.

"Damn you for a liar and a scandalmonger and a malicious old woman!" he shouted, oblivious of many staring coachmen. "Never enter my house again."

But the undaunted Travers steadied himself and replied with a leer, "Well, I made her give herself dead away, whether you like it or not. And it'll be all over town in a week."

Mr. McLane turned his back, and ordering the astonished butler to take out the man's hat and greatcoat, returned to a scene of excitement. Madeleine had been placed full length on a sofa by an open window, and was evidently reviving. He asked the men who had overheard Travers' attack to follow him to his study.

"I want every one of you to promise me that you will not repeat what that little brute said," he commanded. "Fortunately there were no women about. Fainting women are no novelty. And if that cur tells the story of his dastardly assault, give him the lie. Swear that he never said it. Persuade him that he was too drunk to remember."

"I'll follow him and threaten to horsewhip him if he opens his mouth!" cried Colonel Belmont, who had been a dashing cavalry officer during the war. He revered all women of his own class, even his wife, who rarely saw him; and he was so critical of feminine perfections of any sort that he changed his mistresses oftener than any man in San Francisco. "I'll not lose a moment." And he left the room as if charging the enemy.

"Good. Will the rest of you promise?"

"Of course we'll promise."

But alas, wives have means of extracting secrets when their suspicions are alert and clamoring that no husband has the wit to elude, man being too ingenuous to follow the circumlocutory methods of the subtler sex. Not that there was ever anything subtle about Mrs. Abbott's methods. Mr. Abbott had a perpetual catarrh and it had long since weakened his fibre. It was commonly believed that when Mrs. Abbott, her large bulk arrayed in a red flannel nightgown, sat up in the connubial bed and threatened to pour hot mustard up his nose unless he opened his sluices of information he ingloriously succumbed.

At all events, how or wherefore, Travers' prediction was fulfilled, although he shiveringly held his own tongue. The story was all over town not in a week but in three days. But of this Madeleine knew nothing. The doctor, who feared typhoid fever, ordered her to keep quiet and see no one until he discovered what was the matter with her. Her return to Society and Masters' to San Francisco coincided, but at least her little world knew that Dr. Talbot had been responsible for her retirement. It awaited future developments with a painful and a pleasurable interest.

XX

The rest of the season, however, passed without notable incident. But it was known that Madeleine saw Masters constantly, and she was so narrowly observed during his second absence that the nervousness it induced made her forced gaiety almost hysterical. During the late spring her spirits grew more even and her migraines less frequent; sustained as she was by the prospect of her old uninterrupted relations with Masters.

But more than Mrs. Abbott divined the cause of her ill-suppressed expectancy and never had she received so many invitations to the country. Mrs. McLane spent her summers at Congress Springs, but even she pressed Madeleine to visit her. Sally Abbott lived across the Bay on Lake Merritt and begged for three days a week at least; while as for Mrs. Abbott and Mr. and Mrs. Tom, who lived with her, they would harken to no excuses.

Madeleine was almost nonplussed, but if her firm and graceful refusals to leave the doctor had led to open war she would have accepted the consequences. She was determined that this summer she had lived for throughout seven long tormented months should be as unbroken and happy as the other fates would permit. She had a full presentiment that it would be the last.

Masters glided immediately into the old habit and saw her oftener when he could. Of course no phase ever quite repeats itself. The blithe unconsciousness of that first immortal summer was gone for ever; each was playing a part and dreading lest the other suspect it. Moreover, Masters was irritated almost beyond endurance at the constant postponement of the financial equipment for his newspaper. The man who had promised the largest contribution had died suddenly, and although his heir was more than eager to be associated with so illustrious an enterprise he must await the settlement of the estate.

"I am beginning to believe I never shall have that newspaper," Masters said gloomily to Madeleine. "It looks like Fate. When the subject was first broached there was every prospect that I should get the money at once. It has an ugly look. Any man who has been through a war is something of a fatalist."

They were less circumspect than of old and were walking out the old Mission Road. In such moods it was impossible for him to idle before a fire and read aloud. Madeleine had told her husband she would like to join Masters in his walks occasionally, and he had replied heartily: "Do you good. He'll lead you some pretty tramps! I can't keep up with him. You don't walk half enough. Neither do these other women, although my income would be cut in half if they did."

It was a cool bracing day without dust or wind and Madeleine had started out in high spirits, induced in part by a new and vastly becoming walking suit of forest green poplin and a hat of the same shade rolled up on one side and trimmed with a drooping grey feather. Her gloves and shoes were of grey suede, there was soft lace about her white throat and a coquettish little veil that covered only her eyes.

She always knew what to say when Masters was in one of his black moods, and today she reminded him of the various biographies of great men they had read together. Had not all of them suffered every disappointment and discouragement in the beginning of their careers? Overcome innumerable obstacles? Many had been called upon to endure grinding poverty as well until they forced recognition from the world, and he at least was spared that. If Life took with one hand while she gave with the other, the reverse was equally true; and also no doubt it was a part of her beneficence that she not only strengthened the character by preliminary hardships, but amiably planned them that success might be all the sweeter when it came.

Masters laughed. "Incontrovertible. Mind you practice your own philosophy when you need it. All reverses should be temporary if people are strong enough."

She lost her color for a moment, but answered lightly: "That is an easy philosophy for you. If one thing failed you would simply move on to another. Men like you never really fail, for your rare abilities give you the strength and resource of ten men."

"I wonder! The roots of strength sometimes lie in slimy and corrupting waters that spread their miasma upward when Life frowns too long and too darkly. Sometimes misfortunes pile up so remorselessly, this miasma whispers that a man's chief strength consists in going straight to the devil and be done with it all. A resounding slap on Life's face. An insolent assertion of the individual will against Society. Or perhaps it is merely a disposition to run full tilt, hoping for the coup de grace - much as I felt when I lay neglected on the battlefield for twenty-four hours and longed for some Yank to come along and blow out my brains."

"That is no comparison," she said scornfully. "When the body is whole nothing is impossible. I should feel that the Universe was reeling if I saw you go down before adversity. I could as readily imagine myself letting go, and I am only a woman."

"Oh, I should never fear for you," he said bitterly. "What with your immutable principles, your religion, and your proud position in the Society of San Francisco to sustain you, you would come through the fiery furnace unscathed."

"Yes, but the furnace! The furnace!"

She threw out her hands with a gesture of despair, her high spirits routed before a sudden blinding vision of the future. "Does any woman ever escape that?"

One of her hands brushed his and he caught it irresistibly. But he dropped it at once. There was a sound of horses' hoofs behind them. He had been vaguely aware of cantering hoof-beats in the distance for several minutes.

Two men passed, and one of them took off his hat with a low mocking sweep and bowed almost to the saddle. It was old Ben Travers.

"What on earth is he doing in town?" muttered Masters in exasperation. No one had told him of the New Year's Day episode, but he knew him for what he was.

Madeleine was fallowing the small trim figure on the large chestnut with expanded eyes, but she answered evenly enough: "He has some ailment and is remaining in town under Howard's care."

"Liver, no doubt," said Masters viciously. "Too bad his spleen doesn't burst once for all."

He continued unguardedly, "Well, if he tries to make mischief, Howard will tell him bluntly that we walk together with his permission and invite him to go to the devil."

Her own guard was up at once, although it was not any gossip carried to Howard she feared. "He has probably already forgotten us," she said coldly. "Have you finished that paper for *Putnam's?*"

"Three days ago, and begun another for the *Edinburgh Review*. That is the first time I have been invited to write for an English review."

"You see!" she cried gaily. "You are famous already. And ambitious! You were once thinking of writing for our *Overland Monthly* only. Bret Harte told me you had promised him three papers this year."

"I shall write them."

"Perfunctory patriotism. You'd have to write the entire magazine and bring it out weekly to get rid of all your ideas and superfluous energy."

"Well, and wouldn't the good Californians rather read any magazine but their own? Even Harte is far better known in the East than here. I doubt if I've heard one of his things mentioned but 'The Heathen Chinee.' He has been here so long they regard him as a mere native. If I am advancing my reputation in the East I am making it much faster than if I depended upon the local reputation alone. San Francisco is remarkably human."

"When I first came here - it seems a lifetime ago! - I never saw an Eastern magazine of the higher class and rarely a book. I believe you have done as much to wake them up as even the march of time. They read newspapers if they won't read their own poor little *Overland*. And you are popular personally and inspire a sort of uneasy emulation. You are a sort of illuminated bridge. Now tell me what your new paper is about."

XXI

A while later they came to the old Mission Dolores, long ago the center of a flourishing colony of native Indians, who, under the driving energy of the padres, manufactured practically every simple necessity known to Spain. There was nothing left but the crumbling church and its neglected graveyard, alone in a waste of sand. The graves of the priests and grandees were overrun with periwinkle, and the only other flower was the indestructible Castilian rose. The heavy dull green bushes with their fluted dull pink blooms surrounded by tight little buds, were as dusty as the memory of the Spaniard in California.

They went into the church to rest. Madeleine had never taken any interest in the history of her adopted state, and as they sat in a pew at the back, surrounded by silence and a deep twilight gloom, Masters told her the tragic story of Rezanov and Concha Arguello, who would have married before that humble altar and the history of California changed if the ironic fates had permitted. The story had been told him by Mrs. Hathaway, who was the daughter of one of the last of the grandees, and whose mother had lived in the Presidio when Rezanov sailed in through the Golden Gate and Concha Arguello had been La Favorita of Alta California.

The little church was very quiet. The rest of the world seemed far away. Madeleine's fervid yielding imagination swept her back to that long-forgotten past when a woman to whom the earlier fates had been as kind as to herself had scaled all but the highest peaks of happiness and descended into the profoundest depths of despair. Her sympathies, enhanced by her own haunting premonition of disaster, shattered her guard. She dropped her head into her hands and wept hopelessly. Masters felt his own moorings shake. He half rose to flee. But he too had been living in the romantic and passionate past and he too had been visited by moments of black forebodings. Love had tormented him to the breaking point before this and his ambition had often been submerged in his impatience for the excess of work which his newspaper would demand, exhausting to body and imagination alike. He had long ceased to doubt that she loved him, but her self-command had protected them both. He had believed it would never desert her and when it did his pulses had their way. He took her in his arms and strained her to him as if with the strength of his muscles and his will he would defy the blundering fates.

Madeleine made no resistance. She was oblivious of everything but the ecstasy of the moment. When he kissed her she clung to him as ardently, and felt as mortals may, when, in dissolution, they have the vision of unmortal bliss. She had the genius for completion and neither the past nor the future intruded upon the perfect moment when love was all.

But the moment was brief. A priest entered and knelt before the altar. She disengaged herself and adjusted her hat with hands that trembled violently, then almost ran out of the church. Masters followed her. As they

Gertrude Atherton

descended the steps Travers and his companion passed again, after their short canter down the peninsula. He stared so hard at Madeleine's revealing face that he almost forgot to take off his hat, and half reined in as if he would pause and gratify his curiosity; but thought better of it and rode on.

Masters and Madeleine did not exchange a word until they had walked nearly a mile. But his brain was working as clearly as if passion had never clouded it, and although he could see no hope for the future he was determined to gain time and sacrifice anything rather than lose what little he might still have of her. He said finally, in a matter-of-fact voice:

"I want you to use your will and imagination and forget that we ever entered that church."

"Forget! The memory of it will scourge me as long as I live. I have been unfaithful to my husband!"

"Oh, not quite as bad as that!"

"What difference? I had surrendered completely and forgotten my vows, my religion, every principle that has guided my life. If - if - circumstances had been different that would not have been the end. I am a bad wicked woman."

"Oh, no, you are not. You are a terribly good one. If you were not you would take your life in your hands and make it over."

He did not dare mention the word divorce, and lest it travel from his mind to hers and cause his immediate repudiation, he added hastily:

"You were immortal for a moment and it should be your glory, not a whip to scourge you. The time will come when you will remember it with gratitude and without a blush. You know now what you could be and feel. If we part at least you will have been saved from the complete aridity -"

"Part?" She looked at him for the first time, and although she had believed she never could look at him again without turning scarlet, there was only terror in her eyes.

"I have been afraid of banishment."

"It was my fault as much as yours."

"I am not so sure. We won't argue that point. Is anything perfect arguable? But if I am to stay in San Francisco I must see you."

"I'll never see you alone again."

"I have no intention of pressing that point! But the open is safe and you must walk with me every day."

"I don't know! Oh - I don't know! And I think that I should tell Howard."

"You will not tell Howard because you are neither cowardly nor cruel. Nor will you ruin a perfect memory that belongs to us alone. You do love me and that is the end of it - or the beginning of God knows what!"

"Love!" She shivered. "Yes, I love you. Why do poets waste so many beautiful words over love? It is the most terrible thing in the world."

"Let us try to forget it for the present," he said harshly. "Forget everything we cannot have -"

"You have your work. You have only to work harder than ever. What have I?"

"We will walk together every day. We can take a book out on the beach and sit on the rocks. Read more fiction. That is its mission - to translate one for a time from the terrible realities of life. Your religion should be of some use to you. It is almost a pity there is no poverty out here. Sink your prejudices and seek out poor Sibyl Forbes. Every woman in town has cut her. In healing her wounds you could forget your own. Above all, use your will. We are neither of us weaklings, and it could be a thousand times worse. Nothing shall take from us what we have, and there may be a way out."

"There is none," she said sadly. "But I will do as you tell me. And I'll forget - not remember - if I can."

XXII

The end came swiftly. The next day Ben Travers drove down to Rincona. Mrs. Abbott listened to his garnished tale with bulging eyes and her three chins quivering with excitement. She had heard no gossip worth mentioning since she left town, and privately she hated the summer and Alta.

"You should have seen her face when she came out of that church," cried Travers for the third time; he was falling into the senile habit of repeating himself. "It was fairly distorted and she looked as if she had been crying for a week. Mark my words, Masters had been making the hottest kind of love to her - he was little more composed than she. Bet you an eagle to a dime they elope within a week."

"Serve Howard Talbot right for marrying a woman twenty years younger than himself and a Northerner to boot. Do you think he suspects?"

"Not he. Now, I must be off. If I didn't call on the Hathaways and Montgomerys while I'm down here they'd never forgive me."

"Both have house parties," said Mrs. Abbott enviously. "Just like you to get it first! I'd go with you but I must write to Antoinette McLane. She'll *have* to believe that her paragon is headed for the rocks this time."

Mrs. McLane was having an attack of the blues when the letter arrived and did not open her mail until two days later. Then she drove at once to San Francisco. She was too wise in women to remonstrate with Madeleine, but she went directly to Dr. Talbot's office. It was the most unpleasant duty she had ever undertaken, but she knew that Talbot would not doubt his wife's fidelity, and she was determined to save Madeleine. She had considered the alternative of going to Masters, but even her strong spirit quailed before the prospect of that interview. Besides, if he were as deeply in love with Madeleine as she believed him to be, it would do no good. She had little faith in the self-abnegation of men where their passions were concerned.

Dr. Talbot was in his office and saw her at once, and they talked for an hour. His face was purple and she feared a stroke. But he heard her quietly, and told her she had proved her friendship by coming to him before it was too late. When she left him he sat for another hour, alone.

XXIII

It was six o'clock. San Francisco was enjoying one of its rare heat waves and Madeleine had put on a frock of white lawn made with a low neck and short sleeves, and tied a soft blue sash round her waist. As the hour of her husband's reasonably prompt homing approached she seated herself at the piano. She could not trust herself to sing, and played the "Adelaide." The past three days had not been as unhappy as she had expected. She had visited Sibyl Forbes, living in lonely splendor, and listened enthralled to that rebellious young woman (who had received her with passionate gratitude) as she poured out humiliations, bitter resentment, and matrimonial felicity. Madeleine had consoled and rejoiced and promised to talk to the all-powerful Mrs. McLane.

Twice she had gone to hear John McCullough at his new California Theatre, with another dutiful doctor's wife who lived in the hotel, and she had walked for three hours with Masters every afternoon. He had always found it easy to turn her mind into any channel he chose, and he had never exerted himself to be more entertaining even with her.

Today he had been jubilant and had swept her with him on his high tide of anticipation and triumph. Another patriotic San Franciscan had come to the rescue and the hundred thousand dollars lay to Masters' credit in the Bank of California. He had taken his offices an hour after the deposit was made; his business manager was engaged, and every writer of ability on the other newspapers was his to command. "Masters' Newspaper" had been the talk of the journalistic world for months. He had picked his staff and he now awaited only the presses he had ordered that morning from New York.

Madeleine had sighed as she listened to him dilate upon an active brilliant future in which she had no place, but she was in tune with him always and she could only be happy with him now. Moreover, it was an additional safeguard. He would be too busy for dreams and human longings. As for herself she would go along somehow. Tears, after all, were a wonderful solace. Fear had driven her down a light romantic by-way of her nature. Even if days passed without a glimpse of him she could dwell on the pleasant thought that he was not far away, and now and then they would take a long walk together.

The door opened and Dr. Talbot entered. His face was no longer purple. It was sallow and drawn. Her hands trailed off the keys, her arms fell limply. Not even during an epidemic, when he found little time for sleep, had his round face lost its ruddy brightness, his black eyes their look of jovial good-fellowship, his mouth its amiable cynicism.

"Something has happened," she said faintly. "What is it?"

"Would you mind sitting here?" He fell heavily into a chair and motioned to one opposite. She left the shelter of the piano with dragging feet, her own face drained of its color. Ben Travers! She knew what was coming.

His arms lay limply along the arms of his chair. As she gazed at him fascinated it seemed to her that he grew older every minute. And she had never seen any one look as sad.

"I have been a bad husband to you," he said. And the life had gone out of even his voice.

"Oh! No! No! you have been the best, the kindest and most indulgent of husbands."

"I have been worse than a bad husband," he went on in the same monotonous voice. "I have been a failure. I never tried to understand you. I didn't want to under-stand what might interfere with my own selfish life. You have a mind and I ordered you to feed it husks. You asked me for the companionship that was your right and I told you to go and amuse yourself as best you could. I fooled myself with the excuse that you were perfect as you were, but the bald truth was that I liked the society of men better, and hated any form of mental exertion unconnected with my profession. I plucked the rarest flower a good-for-nothing man ever found and I didn't even remember to give it fresh water. It is a wonder you didn't wilt before you did. You were wilting - dying mentally - when Masters came along. You found in him all that I had denied you. And now I have the punishment I deserve. You no longer love me. You love him."

"Oh - Oh - " Madeleine twisted her hands in her lap and stared at them. "You - you - cannot help being what you are. I long since ceased to find fault with you -"

"Yes, when you ceased to love me! When you found that we were hopelessly mismated. When you gave up."

"I - I'm very fond of you still. How could I help it when you are so good to me?"

"I have no doubt of your friendship - or of your fidelity. But you love Masters. Can you deny it?"

"No."

"Are you preparing to elope with him?"

"Oh! No! No! How could you dream of such a thing?"

"I am told that every one is expecting it."

"I would no more elope than I would ask for a divorce. I may be sinful enough to love a man who is not my husband, but I am not bad enough for that. And people are very stupid. They know that Langdon Masters' future lies here. If I were as wicked a woman as that, at least he is not a fool. Why, only today he received the capital for his newspaper."

"And do you know so little of men and women as to imagine that you two could go on indefinitely content with the mere fact that you love each other? I may not have known my own wife because I chose to be blind, but a doctor knows as much about women in general as a father confessor. Men and women are not made like that! It seems that every one but myself has known for months that Masters is in love with you; and Masters is a man of strong passions and relentless will. He has used his will so far to curb his passions, principally, no doubt, on my account; he is my friend and a man of honor. But there are moments in life when honor as well as virtue goes overboard."

"But - but - we have agreed never to see each other alone again - except out of doors."

"That is all very well, but there are always unexpected moments of isolation. The devil sees to that. And while I have every confidence in your virtue - under normal conditions - I know the helpless yielding of women and the ruthless passions of men. It would be only a question of time. I may have been a bad husband but I am mercifully permitted to save you, and I shall do so."

He rose heavily from his chair. "Do you know where I can find Masters?"

She sprang to her feet and for the first time in her life her voice was shrill.

"You are not going to kill him?"

"Oh, no. I am not going to kill him. There has been scandal enough already. And I have no desire to kill him. He has behaved very well, all things considered. I am almost as sorry for him as I am for you - and myself! Do you know where he is?"

"He is probably dining at the Union Club - or he may be at his new offices. They are somewhere on Commercial Street."

He went out and Madeleine sat staring at the door with wide eyes and parted lips. She felt no inclination to tears, nor even to faint, although her body could hardly have been colder in death. She felt suspended in a vacuum, awaiting something more dreadful than even this interview with her husband had been.

XXIV

Dr. Talbot turned toward the stairs, but it occurred to him that Masters might still be in his rooms and he walked to the other end of the hall. A ringing voice answered his knock. He entered. Masters grasped him by the hand, exclaiming, "I was going to look you up tonight and tell you the good news. Has Madeleine told you? I have my capital! And I have just received a telegram from New York saying that my presses will start by freight tomorrow. That means we'll have our newspaper in three weeks at the outside - But what is the matter, old chap? I never saw you look seedy before. Suppose we take a week off and go on a bear hunt? It's the last vacation I can have in a month of Sundays."

"I have come to tell you that you must leave San Francisco."

"Oh!" Masters' exuberance dropped like a shining cloak from a figure of steel. He walked to his citadel, the hearth rug, and lit a cigarette.

"I suppose you have been listening to the chatter of that infernal old gossip, Ben Travers."

"Ben Travers knows me too well to bring any of his gossip to me. But he has carried his stories up and down the state; not only his - more recent discoveries, but evidence he appears to have been collecting for months. But he is only one of many. It seems the whole town has known for a year or more that you see Madeleine for three or four hours every day, that you have managed to have those hours together, no matter what her engagements, that you are desperately in love with each other. The gossip has been infernal. I do not deny that a good deal of the blame rests on my shoulders. I not only neglected her but I encouraged her to see you. But I thought her above scandal or even gossip, and I never dreamed it was in her to love - to lose her head over any man. She was sweet and affectionate but cold - my fault again. Any man who had the good fortune to be married to Madeleine could make her love him if he were not a selfish fool. Well, I have been punished; but if I have lost her I can save her - and her reputation. You must go. There is no other way."

"That is nonsense. You exaggerate because you are suffering from a shock. You know that I cannot leave San Francisco with this great newspaper about to be launched. If it is as bad as you make out I will give you my word not to see Madeleine again. And as I shall be too busy for Society it will quickly forget me."

"Oh, no, it will not. It will say that you are both cleverer than you have been in the past. If you leave San Francisco - California - for good and all - it may forget you; not otherwise."

"Do you know that you are asking me to give up my career? That I shall never have such an opportunity in my life again? My whole future - for usefulness as well as for the realization of my not ignoble ambitions - lies in San Francisco and nowhere else?"

"Don't imagine I have not thought of that. And San Francisco can ill afford to spare you. You are one of the greatest assets this city ever had. But she will have to do without you even if you never can be replaced. I had the whole history of the affair from Mrs. McLane this afternoon. No one believes - yet - that things have reached a climax between you and Madeleine. On the contrary, they are expecting an elopement. But if you remain, nothing on God's earth can prevent an abominable scandal. Madeleine's name will be dragged through the mud. She will be cut, cast out of Society. Even I could not protect her; I should be regarded as a blind fool, or worse, for it will be known that Mrs. McLane warned me. No woman can keep her mouth shut. She and other powerful women - even that damned old cut-throat, Mrs. Abbott - are standing by Madeleine loyally, but they are all alert for a denouement nevertheless. If you go, that will satisfy them. Madeleine will be merely the heroine of an unhappy love-affair, and although nothing will stop their damned clacking tongues for a time, they will pity her and do their best to make her forget."

"I cannot go. It is impossible. You are asking too much. And, I repeat, I'll never see her again. Mrs. McLane can be made to understand the truth. I'll leave the hotel tomorrow."

"You love Madeleine, do you not?"

"Yes - I do."

"Then will you save her from ruin in the only way possible. It is not only her reputation that I fear. You know yourself, I fancy. You may avoid her, but you will hardly deny that if circumstances threw you together, alone, temptation would be irresistible - the more so as you would have ached for the mere sound of her voice every minute. I know now what it means to love Madeleine."

Masters turned his back on Talbot and leaned his arms on the mantel-shelf. He saw hideous pictures in the empty grate.

The doctor had not sat down. Not a muscle of his big strong body had moved as he stood and pronounced what was worse than a sentence of death on Langdon Masters. He averted his dull inexorable eyes, for he dared not give way to sympathy. For the moment he wished himself dead - and for more reasons than one! But he was far too healthy and practical to contemplate a dramatic exit. No end would be served if he did. Madeleine's sensitive spirit would recoil in horror from a union haunted by the memory of the crime and anguish of the husband she had vowed to love and obey. Not Madeleine! His remorseless solution was the only one.

Masters turned after a time and his face looked as old as Talbot's.

"I'll go if you are quite sure it is necessary. If you have not spoken in the heat of the moment."

"If I thought for a month it would make no difference. If you remain, no matter what your circumspection Madeleine will rank in the eyes of the world with those harlots over on Dupont Street. And be as much of an outcast. You know this town. You've lived in it for a year and a half. It's not London, nor even New York. Nothing is hidden here. It lives on itself; it has nothing else to live on. It is almost fanatically loyal to its own until its loyalty is thrown in its face. Then it is bitterer than the wrath of God. You understand all this, don't you?"

"Yes, I understand. But - couldn't you send Madeleine to her parents in Boston for six months - she has never paid them a visit - but no, I suppose the scandal would be worse -"

"Far worse. It would look either as if she had run away from me or as if I had packed her off in disgrace. If I could leave my practice I'd take her abroad for two years, but I cannot. Nor - to be frank - do I see why I should be sacrificed further."

"Oh, assuredly not." Masters' tones were even and excessively polite.

"You will take the train tomorrow morning for New York?"

"I cannot leave San Francisco until after the opening of the banks. The money must be refunded. Besides, I prefer to go by steamer. There is one leaving tomorrow, I believe. I want time to think before I arrive in New York."

"And you will promise to have no correspondence with Madeleine whatever?"

"You might leave us that much!"

"The affair shall end here and now. Do you promise?"

"Very well. But I should like to see her once more."

"That you shall not! I shall not leave her until you are outside the Golden Gate."

"Very well. If that is all -"

"Good-by. You have behaved - well, as our code commands you to behave. I expected nothing less. Don't imagine I don't appreciate what this means to you. But you are a man of great ability. You will find as hospitable a field for your talents elsewhere. San Francisco is the chief loser. I wish you the best of luck."

And he returned to Madeleine.

XXV

Madeleine came of a brave race and she was a woman of intense pride. She spent a week at Congress Springs and she took her courage in her teeth and spent another at Rincona. There was a house party and they amused themselves in the somnolent way peculiar to Alta. Bret Harte was there, a dapper little man, whose shoes were always a size too small, but popular with women as he played an excellent game of croquet and talked as delightfully as he wrote. His good humor could be counted on if no one mentioned "The Heathen Chinee." He had always admired Madeleine and did his best to divert her.

Both Mrs. McLane and Mrs. Abbott were disappointed that they were given no opportunity to condole with her; but although she gave a fair imitation of the old Madeleine Talbot, and even mentioned Masters' name with a casual indifference, no one was deceived for a moment. That her nerves were on the rack was as evident as that her watchful pride was in arms, and although it was obvious that she had foresworn the luxury of tears, her eyes had a curious habit of looking through and beyond these good ladies until they had the uncomfortable sensation that they were not there and some one else was. They wondered if Langdon Masters were dead and she saw his ghost.

The summer was almost over. After a visit to Sally Abbott on Lake Merritt, she returned to town with the rest of the fashionable world. People had never been kinder to her; and if their persistent attentions were strongly diluted with curiosity, who shall blame them? It was not every day they had a blighted heroine of romance, who, moreover, looked as if she were going into a decline. She grew thinner every day. Her white skin was colorless and transparent. They might not have her for long, poor darling! How they pitied her! But they never wished they had let her alone. It was all for the best. And what woman ever had so devoted a husband? He went with her everywhere. He, too, looked as if he had been through the mill, poor dear, but at least he had won a close race, and he deserved and received the sympathy of his faithful friends. As for that ungrateful brute, Langdon Masters, he had not written a line to any one in San Francisco since he left. Not one had an idea what had become of him. Did he secretly correspond with Madeleine? (They would have permitted her that much.) Would he blow out his brains if she died of consumption? He was no philanderer. If he hadn't really loved her nothing would have torn him from San Francisco and his brilliant career; of course. Duelling days were over, and the doctor was not the man to shoot another down in cold blood, with no better excuse than the poor things had given him. It was all very thrilling and romantic. Even the girls talked of little else, and regarded their complacent prosperous swains with disfavor. "The Long Long Weary Day" was their favorite song. They wished that Madeleine lived in a moated grange instead of the Occidental Hotel.

Madeleine had had her own room from the beginning of her married life in San Francisco, as the doctor was frequently called out at night. When Howard had returned and told her that Masters would leave on the morrow and that she was not to see him again, she had walked quietly into her bedroom and locked the door that led to his; and she had never turned the key since.

Talbot made no protest. He had no spirit left where Madeleine was concerned, but it was his humble hope to win her back by unceasing devotion and consideration, aided by time. He not only never mentioned Masters' name, but he wooed her in blundering male fashion. Not a day passed that he did not send her flowers. He bought her trinkets and several valuable jewels, and he presented her with a victoria, drawn by a fine sorrel mare, and a coachman in livery on the box.

Madeleine treated him exactly as she treated her host at a dinner. She was as amiable as ever at the breakfast table, and when he deserted his club of an evening, she sat at her embroidery frame and told him the gossip of the day.

XXVI

One evening at the end of two long hours, when he had heroically suppressed his longing for a game of poker, he said hesitatingly, "I thought you were so fond of reading. I don't see any books about. All the women are reading a novel called 'Quits.' I'll send it up to you in the morning if you haven't read it."

For the first time since Masters' departure the blood rose in Madeleine's face, but she answered calmly:

"Thanks. I have little time for reading, as I have developed quite a passion for embroidery and I practice a good deal. This is a handkerchief-case for Mrs. McLane. Of course I must read 'Quits,' however, and also 'The Initials.' One mustn't be behind the times. If you'll step into Beach's tomorrow and order them I'll be grateful."

"Of course I will. Should - should - you like me to read to you? I'm a pretty bad reader, I guess, but I'll do my best."

"Oh - is there an earthquake?"

"No! But your nerves are in a bad state. I'll get you a glass of port wine."

He went heavily over to the cupboard, but his hand was shaking as he poured out the wine. He drank a glass himself before returning to her.

"Thanks. You take very good care of me." And she gave him the gracious smile of a grateful patient.

"I don't think you'd better go out any more at night for a while. You are far from well, you know, and you're not picking up."

"A call for you, I suppose. Too bad."

There had been a peremptory knock on the door. A coachman stood without. Would Dr. Talbot come at once? A new San Franciscan was imminent via Mrs. Alexander Groome on Ballinger Hill.

The doctor grumbled.

"And raining cats and dogs. Why couldn't she wait until tomorrow? We'll probably get stuck in the mud. Damn women and their everlasting babies."

She helped him into his overcoat and wished him a pleasant good-night. It was long since she had lifted her cheek for his old hasty kiss, and he made no protest. He had time on his side.

She did not return to her embroidery frame but stood for several moments looking at the chest near the fireplace. She had not opened it since Masters left. His library had been packed and sent after him by one of his friends, but no one had known of the books in her possession. Masters certainly had not thought of them and she was in no condition to remember them herself at the time.

She had not dared to look at them! Tonight, however, she moved slowly toward the chest. She looked like a sleep-walker. When she reached it she knelt down and opened it and gathered the books in her arms. When her husband returned two hours later she lay on the floor in a dead faint, the books scattered about her.

XXVII

It was morning before he could revive her, and two days before she could leave her bed. Then she developed the hacking cough he dreaded. He took her to the Sandwich Islands and kept her there for a month. The even climate and the sea voyage seemed to relieve her, but when they returned to San Francisco she began to cough again.

Do women go into a decline these days from corroding love and hope in ruins? If so, one never hears of it and the disease is unfashionable in modern fiction. But in that era woman was woman and little besides. If a woman of the fashionable world she had Society besides her family and housekeeping. She rarely travelled, certainly not from California, and if one of her band fell upon evil days and was forced to teach school, knit baby sacques, or keep a boarding-house, she was pitied but by no means emulated. Madeleine had neither house nor children, and more money than she could spend. She had nothing to ask of life but happiness and that was for ever denied her. Masters had never been out of her mind for a moment during her waking hours, and she had slept little. She ate still less, and kept herself up in Society with punch in the afternoon and champagne at night. Only in the solitude of her room did she give way briefly to excoriated nerves; but the source of her once ready tears seemed dry. There are more scientific terms for her condition these days, but she was poisoned by love and despair. Her collapse was only a matter of time.

Dr. Talbot knew nothing about psychology but he knew a good deal about consumption. He had also arrested it in its earlier stages more than once. He plied Madeleine with the good old remedies: eggnog, a raw egg in a glass of sherry, port wine, mellow Bourbon whiskey and cream. She had no desire to recover and he stood over her while she drank his potions lest she pour them down the washstand; and some measure of her strength returned. She fainted no more and her cough disappeared. The stimulants gave her color and her figure began to fill out again. But her thoughts, save when muddled by her tonics, never wandered from Masters for a moment.

The longing to hear from him grew uncontrollable with her returning vitality. She had hoped that he would break his promise and write to her once at least. He knew her too well not to measure the extent of her sufferings, and common humanity would have justified him. But his ship might have sunk with all on board for any sign he gave. Others had ceased to grumble at his silence; his name was rarely mentioned.

If she had known his address she would have written to him and demanded one letter. She had given no promise. Her husband had commanded and she had obeyed. She had always obeyed him, as she had vowed at the altar. But she had her share of feminine guile, and if she had known where to address Masters she would have quieted her conscience with the assurance that a letter from him was a necessary part of her cure. She felt that the mere sight of his handwriting on an envelope addressed to herself would transport her back to that hour in Dolores, and if she could correspond with him life would no longer be unendurable. But although he had casually alluded to his club in New York she could not recall the name, if he had mentioned it.

She went to the Mercantile Library one day and looked over files of magazines and reviews. His name appeared in none of them. It was useless to look over newspaper files, as editorials were not signed. But he must be writing for one of them. He had his immediate living to make.

What should she do?

As she groped her way down the dark staircase of the library she remembered the newspaper friend, Ralph Holt, who had packed his books - so the chambermaid had informed her casually - and whom she had met once when walking with Masters. He, if any one, would know Masters' address. But how meet him? He did not go in Society, and she had never seen him since. She could think of no excuse to ask him to call. Nor was it possible - to her, at least - to write a note and ask him for information outright.

But by this time she was desperate. See Holt she would, and after a few moments' hard thinking her feminine ingenuity flashed a beacon. Holt was one of the sub-editors of his newspaper and although he had been about to resign and join Masters, no doubt he was on the staff still. Madeleine remembered that Masters had often spoken of a French restaurant in the neighborhood of the *Alta* offices, patronized by newspaper men. The cooking was excellent. He often lunched there himself.

She glanced at her watch. It was one o'clock. She walked quickly toward the restaurant.

XXVIII

She entered in some trepidation. She had never visited a restaurant alone before. And this one was crowded with men, the atmosphere thick with smoke. She asked the fat little proprietor if she might have a table alone, and he conducted her to the end of the room, astonished but flattered. A few women came to the restaurant occasionally to lunch with "their boys," but no such lady of the haut ton as this. A fashionable woman's caprice, no doubt.

Her seat faced the room, and as she felt the men staring at her, she studied the menu carefully and did not raise her eyes until she gave her order. In spite of her mission and its tragic cause she experienced a fleeting satisfaction that she was well and becomingly dressed. She had intended dropping in informally on Sibyl Forbes, still an outcast, in spite of her intercession, and wore a gown of dove-colored cashmere and a hat of the same shade with a long lilac feather.

She summoned her courage and glanced about the room, her eyes casual and remote. Would it be possible to recognize any one in that smoke? But she saw Holt almost immediately. He sat at a table not far from her own. She bowed cordially and received as frigid a response as Mrs. Abbott would have bestowed on Sibyl Forbes.

Madeleine colored and dropped her eyes again. Of course he knew her for the cause of Masters' desertion of the city that needed him, and the disappointment of his own hopes and ambitions. Moreover, she had inferred from his conversation the day they had all walked together for half an hour that he regarded Masters as little short of a god. He was several years younger, he was clever himself, and nothing like Masters had ever come his way. He had declared that the projected newspaper was to be the greatest in America. She had smiled at his boyish enthusiasm, but without it she would probably have forgotten him. She had resented his presence at the time.

Of course he hated her. But she had come too far to fail. He passed her table a few moments later and she held out her hand with her sweetest smile.

"Sit down a moment," she said with her pretty air of command; and although his face did not relax he could do no less than obey.

"I feel more comfortable," she said. "I had no idea I should be the only lady here. But Mr. Masters so often spoke to me of this restaurant that I have always meant to visit it." She did not flutter an eyelash as she uttered Masters' name, and her lovely eyes seemed wooing Holt to remain at her side.

"Heartless, like all the rest of them," thought the young man wrathfully. "Well, I'll give her one straight."

"Have you heard from him lately?" she asked, as the waiter placed the dishes on the table. "He hasn't written to one of his old friends since he left, and I've often wondered what has become of him."

"He's gone to the devil!" said Holt brutally. "And I guess you know where the blame lies - Oh! - Drink this!" He hastily poured out a glass of claret. "Here! Drink it! Brace up, for God's sake. Don't give yourself away before all these fellows."

Madeleine swallowed the claret but pushed back her chair. "Take me away quickly," she muttered. "I don't care what they think. Take me where you can tell me -"

He drew her hand through his arm, for he was afraid she would fall, and as he led her down the room he remarked audibly, "No wonder you feel faint. There's no air in the place, and you've probably never seen so much smoke in your life before."

At the door he nodded to the anxious proprietor, and when they reached the sidewalk asked if he should take her home.

"No. I must talk to you alone. There is a hack. Let us drive somewhere."

He handed her into the hack, telling the man to drive where he liked as long as he avoided the Cliff House Road. Madeleine shrank into a corner and began to cry wildly. He regarded her with anxiety, and less hostility in his bright blue eyes.

"I'm awfully sorry," he said. "I was a brute. But I thought you would know - I thought other things -"

"I knew nothing, but I can't believe it is true. There must be some mistake. He is not like that."

"That's what's happened. You see, his world went to smash. That was the opportunity of his life, and such opportunities don't come twice. He has no capital of his own, and he can't raise money in New York. Besides, he didn't want a newspaper anywhere else. And - and - of-course, you know, newspaper men hear all the talk - he was terribly hard hit. I couldn't help feeling a little sorry for you when I heard you were ill and all the rest; but today you looked as if you had forgotten poor Masters had ever lived - just a Society butterfly and a coquette."

"Oh, I'm not blaming you! Perhaps it is all my fault. I don't know! - But *that*! I can't believe it. I never knew a man with as strong a character. He - he - always could control himself. And he had too much pride and ambition."

"I guess you don't know it, but he had a weak spot for liquor. That is the reason he drank less than the rest of us - and that did show strength of character: that he could drink at all. I only saw him half-seas over once. He told me then he was always on the watch lest it get the best of him. His father drank himself to death after the war, and his grandfather from mere love of his cups. Nothing but a hopeless smash-up, though, would ever have let it get the best of him.... He was terribly high-strung under all that fine repose of his, and although his mind was like polished metal in a way, it was full of quicksilver. When a man like that lets go - nothing left to hold on to - he goes down hill at ten times the pace of an ordinary chap. I - I - suppose I may as well tell you the whole truth. He never drew a sober breath on the steamer and he's been drunk more or less ever since he arrived in New York. Of course he writes - has to - but can't hold down any responsible position. They'd be glad to give him the best salary paid if he'd sober up, but he gets worse instead of better. He's been thrown off two papers already; and it's only because he can write better drunk than most men sober that he sells an article now and again when he has to."

Madeleine had torn her handkerchief to pieces. She no longer wept. Her eyes were wide with horror. He fancied he saw awful visions in them. Fearing she might faint or have hysterics, he hastily extracted a brandy flask from his pocket.

"Do you mind?" he asked diffidently. "Sorry I haven't a glass, but this is the first time I've taken the cork out."

She lifted the flask obediently and took a draught that commanded his respect.

She smiled faintly as she met his wide-eyed regard. "My husband makes me live on this stuff. I was threatened with consumption. It affects me very little, but it helps me in more ways than one."

"Well, don't let it help you too much. I suppose the doctor knows best - but - well, it gets a hold on you when you are down on your luck."

"If it ever 'gets a hold' on me it will because I deliberately wish it to," she said haughtily. "If Langdon Masters - has gone as far as you say, I don't believe it is through any inherited weakness. He has done it deliberately."

"I grant that. And I'm sorry if I offended you -"

"I am only grateful to you. I feel better now and can think a little. Something must be done. Surely he can be saved."

"I doubt it. When a man starts scientifically drinking himself to death nothing can be done when there is nothing better to offer him. May I be frank?"

"I have been frank enough!"

"Masters told me nothing of course, but I heard all the talk. Old Travers let out his part of it in his cups, and news travels from the Clubs like water out of a sieve. We don't publish that sort of muck, but there were innuendoes in that blackguard sheet, *The Boom*. They stopped suddenly and I fancy the editor had a taste of the horsewhip. It wouldn't be the first time.... When Masters sent for me and told me he was leaving San Francisco for good and all, he looked like a man who had been through Dore's Hell - was there still, for that matter. Of course I knew what had happened; if I hadn't I'd have known it the next day when I saw the doctor. He looked bad enough, but nothing to Masters. He had less reason! Of course Masters threw his career to the winds to save your good name. Noblesse oblige. Too bad he wasn't more of a villain and less of a great gentleman. It, might have been better all round. This town certainly needs him."

"If he were not a great gentleman nothing would have happened in the first place," she said with cool pride. "But I asked you if there were no way to save him."

"I can think of only two ways. If your husband would write and ask him to return to San Francisco -"

"He'd never do that."

"Then you might - you might - " He was fair and blushed easily. Being secretly a sentimental youth he was shy of any of the verbal expressions of sentiment; but he swallowed and continued heroically. "You - you - I think you love him. I can see you are not heartless, that you are terribly cut up. If you love him enough you might save him. A man like Masters can quit cold no matter how far he has gone if the inducement is great enough. If you went to New York -"

He paused and glanced at her apprehensively, but although she had gasped she only shook her head sadly.

"I'll never break my husband's heart and the vows I made at the altar, no matter what happens."

"Oh, you good women! I believe you are at the root of more disaster than all the strumpets put together!"

"It may be. I remember he once said something of the sort. But he loved me for what I am and I cannot change myself."

"You could get a divorce."

"I have no ground. And I would not if I had. He knows that."

"No wonder he is without hope! But I don't pretend to understand women. You'll leave him in the gutter then?"

"Don't! - Don't -"

"Well, if he isn't there literally he soon will be. I've seen men of your set in the gutter here when they'd only been on a spree for a week. Take Alexander Groome and Jack Belmont, for instance. And after the gutter it is sometimes the calaboose."

"You are cruel, and perhaps I deserve it. But if you will give me his address I will write to him."

"I wouldn't. He might be too drunk to read your letter, and lose it. Or he might tear it up in a fury. I don't fancy even drink could make Langdon Masters maudlin, and the sight of your handwriting would be more likely to make him empty the bottle with a curse than to awaken tender sentiment. Anyhow, it would be a risk. Some blackguard might get hold of it."

"Very well, I'll not write. Will you tell the man to drive to the Occidental Hotel?"

He gave the order and when he drew in his head she laid her hand on his and said in her sweet voice and with her soft eyes raised to his (he no longer wondered that Masters had lost his head over her), "I want to thank you for the kindness you have shown me and the care you took of me in that restaurant. What you have told me has destroyed the little peace of mind I had left, but at least I'm no longer in the dark. I will confess that I went to that restaurant in the hope of seeing you and learning something about Masters. Nor do I mind that I have revealed myself to you without shame. I have had no confidant throughout all this terrible time and it has been a relief. I suppose it is always easier to be frank with a stranger than with even the best of friends."

"Thanks. But I'd like you to know that I am your friend. I'd do anything I could for you - for Masters' sake as well as your own. It's an awful mess. Perhaps you'll think of some solution."

"I've thought of one as far as I am concerned. I shall drink myself to death."

"What?" He was sitting sideways, embracing his knees, and he just managed to save himself from toppling over. "Have you gone clean out of your head?"

"Oh, no. Not yet, But I shall do as I said. If I cannot follow him I can follow his example. Why should he go to the dogs and I go through life with the respect and approval of the world? He is far greater than I - and better. I can at least share his disgrace, and I shall also forget - and, it may be, delude myself that I am with him at times."

"My God! The logic of women! How happy do you think *that* will make your husband? Good old sport, the doctor - and as for religion - and vows!"

"One can stand so much and no more. I have reached the breaking point here in this carriage. It is that or suicide, and that would bring open disgrace on my husband. The other would only be suspected. And I'll not last long."

The hack stopped in front of the hotel. She gave him her hand after he had escorted her to the door. "Thank you once more. And I'd be grateful if you would come and tell me if you have any further news of him - no matter what. Will you?"

"Yes," he said. "But I feel like going off and getting drunk, myself. I wish I hadn't told you a thing."

"It wouldn't have made much difference. If you know it others must, and I'd have heard it sooner or later. I hope you'll call in any case."

He promised; but the next time he saw her it was not in a drawing-room.

XXIX

Madeleine had reached the calmness of despair once more, and this time without a glimmer of hope. Life had showered its gifts sardonically upon her before breaking her in her youth, and there was still a resource in its budget that it had no power to withhold. She was a firm believer in the dogmas of the Church and knew that she would be punished hereafter. Well, so would he. It might be they would be permitted to endure their punishment together. And meanwhile, there was oblivion, delusions possibly, and then death.

It was summer and there were no engagements to break. The doctor was caught in the whirlwind of another small-pox epidemic and lived in rooms he reserved for the purpose. He did not insist upon her departure from town as he knew her to be immune, and he thought it best she should remain where she could pursue her regimen uninterrupted; and tax her strength as little as possible. If he did not dismiss her from his mind at least he had not a misgiving. She had never disobeyed him, she appeared to have forgotten Masters at last, she took her tonics automatically, and there were good plays in town. In a few months she would be restored to health and himself.

He returned to the hotel at the end of six weeks. It was the dinner hour but his wife was not at the piano. He tapped on the door that led from the parlor to her bedroom, and although there was no response he turned the knob and entered.

Madeleine was lying on the bed, asleep apparently.

He went forward anxiously; he had never known her to sleep at this hour before. He touched her lightly on the shoulder, but she did not awaken. Then he bent over her, and drew back with a frown. But although horrified he was far from suspecting the whole truth. He had been compelled to break more than one patient of too ardent a fidelity to his prescriptions.

He forced an emetic down her throat, but it had no effect. Then he picked her up and carried her into the bath room and held her head under the shower. The blood flowed down from her congested brain. She struggled out of his arms and looked at him with dull angry eyes.

"What do you mean?" she demanded. "How dared you do such a thing to me?"

"You had taken too much, my dear," he said kindly. "Or else it affects you more than it did - possibly because you no longer need it. I shall taper you off by degrees, and then I think we can do without it."

"Without it? I couldn't live without it. I need more - and more -" She looked about wildly.

"Oh, that is all right. They always think so at first. In six months you will have forgotten it. Remember, I am a doctor - and a good one, if I say so myself."

She dropped her eyes. "Very well," she said humbly. "Of course you know best."

"Now, put on dry clothes and let us have dinner. It seems a year since I dined with you."

"I haven't the strength."

He went into the parlor and returned with a small glass of cognac. "This will brace you up, and, as I said, you must taper off. But I'll measure the doses myself, hereafter."

She put on an evening gown, but with none of her old niceness of detail. She merely put it on. Her wet hair she twisted into a knot without glancing at the mirror. As she entered the parlor she staggered slightly. Talbot averted his eyes. He may have had similar cases, and, as a doctor, become hardened to all manifestations of human weakness, but this patient was his wife. It was only temporary, of course, and a not unnatural sequel. But Madeleine! He felt as a priest might if a statue of the Virgin opened its mouth and poured forth a stream of blasphemy.

Then he went forward and put his arm about her. "Brace up," he said. "I hear the waiters in the dining-room. They must not see you like this. Where - where have you taken your meals?"

"In my bedroom."

"I hoped so. Has any one seen you?"

"I don't know - no. I think not. I have been careful enough. I do not wish to disgrace you."

He was obliged to give her another glass of cognac, and she sat through the dinner without betraying herself, although she would eat nothing. She was sullen and talked little, and when the meal was over she went directly to bed.

Dr. Talbot followed her, however, and searched her wardrobe and bureau drawers. He found nothing. When he returned to the parlor he locked the cupboard where he kept his hospitable stores and put the key in his pocket. But he did not go out, and toward midnight he heard her moving restlessly about her room. She invited him eagerly to enter when he tapped.

"I'm nervous, horribly nervous," she said. "Give me some more cognac - anything."

"You'll have nothing more tonight. I shall give you a dose of valerian."

She swallowed the noxious mixture with a grimace and was asleep in a few moments.

XXX

The doctor was still very busy but he returned to the hotel four times a day and gave her small doses of whatever liquor she demanded. In a short time he diluted them with Napa Soda water. She was always pacing the room when he entered and looked at him like a wild animal at bay. But she never mentioned Masters' name, even when her nerves whipped her suddenly to hysterics; and although he sometimes thought he should go mad with the horror of it all, he had faith in his method, and in her own pride, as soon as the first torments wore down. She refused to walk out of doors or to wear anything but a dressing gown; she took her slender meals in her room.

But Madeleine's sufferings were more mental than physical, although she was willing the doctor should form the natural conclusion. She was possessed by the fear that a cure would be forced upon her; she was indifferent even to the taste of liquor, and had merely preferred it formerly to bitter or nauseous tonics; in Society it had been a necessary stimulant, when her strength began to fail, nothing more. After her grim decision she had forced large quantities down her throat by sheer strength of will. But she had found the result all that she had expected, she had alternated between exhilaration and oblivion, and was sure that it was killing her by inches. Now, she could indulge in neither wild imaginings nor forget. And if he cured her! - but her will when she chose to exert it was as strong as his, and her resource seldom failed her.

One day in her eternal pacing she paused and stared at the keyhole of the cupboard, then took a hairpin from her head and tried to pick the lock. It was large and complicated and she could do nothing with it. She glanced at the clock. The doctor would not return for an hour. She dressed hastily and went out and bought a lump of soft wax. She took an impress of the keyhole and waited with what patience she could summon until her husband had come and gone. Then she went out again. The next day she had the key and that night she needed no valerian.

Doctor Talbot paced the parlor himself until morning. But he did not despair. He had had not dissimilar experiences before. He removed his supplies to the cellar of the hotel and carried a flask in his pocket from which he measured her daily drams.

The same chambermaid had been on her floor for years, and was devoted to her. She sent her out for gin on one pretext or another, although the woman was not deceived for a moment; she had "seen how it was" long since. But she was middle-aged, Irish, and sympathetic. If the poor lady had sorrows let her drown them.

Madeleine was more wary this time. She told her husband she was determined to take her potions only at noon and at night; in the daytime she restrained herself after four o'clock, although she took enough to keep up her spirits at the dinner-table to which she had thought it best to return.

The doctor, thankful, no longer neglected his practice, and left immediately after dinner for the Club as she went to her room at once and locked the door. There was no doubt of her hostility, but that, too, was not unnatural, and he was content to wait.

Society returned to town, but she flatly refused to enter it. Nor would she receive any one who called. The doctor remonstrated in vain. He trusted her perfectly and a glass of champagne at dinner would not hurt her. If she expected to become quite herself again she must have diversions. She was leading an unnatural life.

She deigned no answer.

He warned her that tongues would wag. He had met several of the women during the summer and told them her lungs were healed.... No doubt he had been over-anxious, mistaken - in the beginning. He wished he had given her a tonic of iron arsenic and strychnine, alternated with cod-liver oil. But it was too late for regrets, and at least she was well on the road to recovery; if she snubbed people now they would take their revenge when she would be eager for the pleasures of Society again.

Madeleine laughed aloud.

"But, my dear, this is only a passing phase. Of course your system is depressed but that will wear off, and what you need now, even more than brandy twice a day, is a mental tonic. By the way, don't you think you might leave it off now?"

"No, I do not. If my system is depressed I'd go to pieces altogether without it."

"I'll give you a regular tonic -"

"I'll not take it. You are not disposed to use force, I imagine."

"No, I cannot do that. But you'll accept these invitations - some of them?" He indicated a pile of square envelopes on the table. He had opened them but she had not given them a passing glance.

"Society would have the effect of arresting my 'cure.' I hate it. If you force me to go out I'll drink too much and disgrace you."

"But what shall I tell them?" he asked in despair. "I see some of them every day and they'll quiz my head off. They can't suspect the truth, of course, but - but - " he paused and his ruddy face turned a deep brick red. He had never mentioned Masters' name to her since he announced his impending departure, but he was desperate. "They'll think you're pining, that's what! That you won't go out because you take no interest in any one but Langdon Masters."

She was standing by the window with her back to him, looking down into the street. She turned and met his eyes squarely.

"That would be quite true," she said.

"You do not mean that!"

"I have never forgotten him for a moment and I never shall as long as I live." She averted her eyes from his pallid face but went on remorselessly. "If you had been merciful you would have let me die when I was so ill.

But you showed me another way, and now you would take even that from me."

"Do - do you mean to say that you tried to drink yourself to death?"

"Yes, I mean that. And if you really cared for me you would let me do it now."

"That I'll never do," he cried violently. "I'll cure you and you'll get over this damned nonsense in time."

"I never shall get over it. Don't delude yourself for an instant."

He stared at her with a sickening sense of impotence - and despair. He thought she had never looked more beautiful. She wore a graceful wrapper of pale blue camel's hair and her long hair in two pendent braids. She was very white and she looked as cold and remote as the moon.

"Madeleine! Madeleine! You have changed so completely! I cannot believe that you'll never be the same Madeleine again. Why - you - you look as if you were not there at all!"

"Only my shell is here. The real me is with him."

"Curse the man! Curse him! Curse him! I wish I'd blown out his brains!" He threw his arms about wildly and she wondered if he would strike her. But he threw himself into a chair and burst into heavy sobbing. Madeleine ran out of the room.

XXXI

"I tell you it's true. You needn't pooh-pooh at me, Antoinette McLane. I have it on the best authority."

"Old Ben Travers, I suppose!"

"No, it's not Ben Travers, although he'll find it out soon enough. Her chambermaid knows my cook. She is devoted to Madeleine, evidently, and cried after she had told it, but - well, I suppose it was too good for any mere female to keep."

"Servants' gossip," replied Mrs. McLane witheringly. "I should think it would be beneath your self-respect to listen to it. Fancy gossiping with one's cook."

"I didn't," replied Mrs. Abbott with dignity. "She told my maid, and if we didn't listen to our maids' gossip how much would we really know about what goes on in this town?"

Mrs. McLane, Mrs. Ballinger, Guadalupe Hathaway and Sally Abbott were sitting in Mrs. Abbott's large and hideous front parlor after luncheon, and she had tormented them throughout the meal with a promise of "something that would make their hair stand on end."

She had succeeded beyond her happy expectations.

Mrs. McLane's eyes were flashing. Mrs. Ballinger looked like a proud silver poplar that had been seared by lightning. Sally burst into tears, and Miss Hathaway's large cold Spanish blue eyes saw visions of Nina Randolph, a brilliant creature of the early sixties, whom she had tried to save from the same fate.

"Be sure the bell boys will find it out," continued Mrs. Abbott unctuously. "And when it gets to the Union Club - well, no use for us to try to hush it up."

"As you are trying to do now!"

"You needn't spit fire at me. I feel as badly as you do about it. If I've told just you four it's only to talk over what can be done."

"I don't believe there's a word of truth in the story. Probably that wretched servant is down on her for some reason. Madeleine Talbot! Why, she's the proudest creature that ever lived."

"She might have the bluest blood of the South in her veins," conceded Mrs. Ballinger handsomely. "I pride myself on my imagination but I simply cannot *see* her in such a condition."

"If it's true, it's Masters, of course," said Miss Hathaway. "The only reason I didn't fall in love with him was because it was no use. But he's the sort of man - there are not many of them! - who would make a woman love him to desperation if he loved her himself. And she'd never forget him."

"I don't believe it," said Mrs. Ballinger coldly. "I never believed that Madeleine was in love with Langdon

Masters. A good woman loves only her husband."

"Oh, mamma!" wailed Sally. "Madeleine is young, and the doctor's a dear but he wasn't the sort of a man for her at all. He just attracted her when she was a girl because he was so different from the men she knew. But Langdon is exactly suited to her. I guessed it before any of you did. It worried me dreadfully, but I sympathized - I always admired Langdon - if he'd looked at me before I fell in love with Hal I believe I'd have married him - but I wish, oh, how I wish, Madeleine could get a divorce."

"Sally Ballinger!" Her mother's voice quavered. "This terrible California! If you had been brought up in Virginia -"

"But I wasn't. And I mean what I say. And - and - it's true about Madeleine. I went there the other day and she saw me - and - oh, I never meant to tell it - it's too terrible!"

"So," said Mrs. McLane. "So," She added thoughtfully after a moment. "It's a curious coincidence. Langdon Masters is drinking himself to death in New York. Jack Belmont returned the other day - he told Mr. McLane."

She had been interrupted several times, Madeleine for the moment forgotten.

"Why didn't Alexander Groome know? He's his cousin and bad enough himself, heaven knows."

"Oh, poor Langdon! Poor Langdon! I knew he could love a woman like that -"

"He has remarkable powers of concentration!"

"I'll wager Mr. Abbott heard it himself at the Club, the wretch! He'll hear from me!"

"Oh, it's too awful," wailed Sally again. "What an end to a romance. It was quite perfect before - in a way. And now instead of pitying poor Madeleine and wishing we were her - she - which is it? - we'll all be despising her!"

"It's loathsome," said Mrs. Ballinger. "I wish I had not heard it. I prefer to believe that such things do not exist."

"Good heavens, mamma, I've heard that gentlemen in the good old South were as drunk as lords, oftener than not."

"As lords, yes. Langdon Masters is in no position to emulate his ancestors. And Madeleine! No one ever heard of a lady in the South taking to drink from disappointed love or anything else. When life was too hard for them they went into a beautiful decline and died in the odor of sanctity."

"They get terribly skinny and yellow in the last stages - "

"Sally!"

"Well, I don't care anything about Langdon Masters," announced Mrs. Abbott. "He's left here anyway, and like as not we'll never see him again. This is what I want to know: Can anything be done about Madeleine Talbot? Of course Howard poured whiskey down her throat until it got the best of her. But he should know how to cure her. That is if he knows the worst."

"You may be sure he knows the worst," said Mrs. McLane. "How could he help it?"

"That maid said she bought it on the sly all the time. Don't you suppose he'd put a stop to that if he knew it?"

"Well, he will find it out. And I'll not be the one to tell him. One ordeal of that sort is enough for a lifetime."

"Why not give her a talking to? She has always seemed to defer more to you than to any one else." Mrs. Abbott made the admission grudgingly.

"I am willing to try, if she will see me. But - if she knows what has happened to Masters - and ten to one she does - he may have written to her - I don't believe it will do any good. Alas! Why does youth take life so tragically? When she is as old as I am she will know that no man is worth the loss of a night's sleep."

"Yes, but Madeleine isn't old!" cried Sally. "She's young - young - and she can't live without him. I don't know whether she's weaker or stronger than Sibyl, but at any rate Sibyl is happy -"

"How do you know?"

"Can't you see it in her face at the theatre? Oh, I don't care! I'll tell it! Madeleine asked me to lunch to meet her one day last winter and I went. We had a splendid time. After lunch we sat on the rug before the fire and popped corn. Oh, you needn't all glare at me as if I'd committed a crime. It's hard to *be* hard when you're young, and Sibyl was my other intimate friend. But that's not the question at present. I've had an idea. Perhaps I could persuade Madeleine to stay with me. Now that I know, perhaps she won't mind so much. I only got in by accident. There's a new man at the desk and he let me go up -"

"Well, what is your idea?" asked Mrs. McLane impatiently. "What could you do with her if she did visit you - which she probably will not."

"I might be able to cure her. She wouldn't see anything to drink. Hal has sworn off. There's not a drop in sight, and not only on his account but because the last butler got drunk and fell in the lake. We'll not have any company while she's there. And I'd lock her in at night and never leave her alone in the daytime."

"That is not a bad idea at all," said Mrs. McLane emphatically. "But don't waste your time trying to persuade her. Go to Howard. Tell him the truth. He will give her a dose of valerian and take her over in a hack at night."

"I don't like the idea of Sally coming into contact with such a dreadful side of life -"

"But if I can save her, mamma?"

"Maria is Alexander Groome's wife and she has no influence over him."

"Oh, Maria! If he were my husband I'd lead him such a dance that he'd behave himself in self-defence. Maria is too much like you -"

"Sally Ballinger!"

"I only meant that you are an angel, mamma dear. And of course you are so enchanting and beautiful papa has always toed the mark. But Maria is good without being any too fascinating -"

"Sally is right," interrupted Mrs. McLane. "I am not sure that her plan will succeed. But no one has thought of a better. If Madeleine has a deeper necessity for stupefying her brain than shattered nerves, I doubt if any one could save her. But at least Sally can try. We'd be brutes if we left her to drown without throwing her a plank."

"Just what I said," remarked Mrs. Abbott complacently. "Was I not justified in telling you? And when you get her over there, Sally, and her mind is quite clear, warn her that while she may do what she chooses in private, if she elects to die that way, just let her once be seen in public in a state unbecoming a lady, and that is the end of her as far as we are concerned."

"Yes," said Mrs. McLane with a sigh. "We should have no choice. Poor Madeleine!"

XXXII

Madeleine awoke from a heavy drugged sleep and reached out her hand automatically for the drawer of her commode. It fumbled in the air for a moment and then she raised herself on her elbow. She glanced about the room. It was not her own.

She sprang out of bed. A key turned and Sally Abbott entered.

"What does this mean?" cried Madeleine. "What are you doing here, Sally? Why did Howard move me into another room?"

"He didn't. You are over at my house. He thought the country would be good for you for a while and I was simply dying to have you -"

"Where are my clothes? I am going back to the city at once."

"Now, Madeleine, dear." Sally put her arm round the tall form which was as rigid as steel in her embrace. But she was a valiant little person and strong with health and much life in the open. "You are going to stay with me until - until - you are better."

Gertrude Atherton

"I'll not. I must get back. At once! You don't understand -"

"Yes, I do. And I've something for you." She took a flask from the capacious pocket of her black silk apron and poured brandy into a glass.

Madeleine drank it, then sank heavily into a chair.

"That is more than he has been giving me," she said suspiciously. "How often did he tell you to give me that?"

"Four times a day."

"He's found out! He's found out!"

"That chambermaid blabbed, and of course he heard it. I - I - saw him just after. He felt so terribly, Madeleine dear! Your heart would have ached for him. And when I asked him to let you come over here he seemed to brighten up, and said it was the best thing to do."

Madeleine burst into tears, the first she had shed in many months. "Poor Howard! Poor Howard! But it will do no good."

"Oh, yes, it will. Now, let me help you dress. Or would you rather stay in bed today?"

"I'll dress. And I'm not going to stay, Sally. I give you fair warning."

"Oh, but you are. I've locked up your outdoor things - and my own! I'll only let you have them when we go out together."

"So you have turned yourself into my jailer?"

"Yes, I have. And don't try to look like an outraged empress until your stays are covered up. Put on your dress and we'll have a game of battledore and shuttle-cock in the hall. It's raining. Then we'll have some music this afternoon. My alto used to go beautifully with your soprano, and I'll get out our duets. I haven't forgotten one of the accompaniments - What are you doing?"

Madeleine was undressing rapidly. "I haven't had my bath. I seldom forget that, even - where is the bath room? I forget."

"Across the hall. And leave your clothes here. Although you'd break your bones if you tried to jump out of the window. When you've finished I'll have a cup of strong coffee ready for you. Run along."

XXXIII

Lake Merritt, a small sheet of water near the little town of Oakland, was surrounded by handsome houses whose lawns sloped down to its rim. Most them were closed in summer, but a few of the owners, like the Harold Abbotts, lived there the year round. At all times, however, the lawns and gardens were carefully tended, for this was one of Fashion's chosen spots, and there must be no criticism from outsiders in Oakland. The statues on the lawns were rubbed down after the heavy rains and dusted as carefully in summer. There were grape-vine arbors and wild rose hedges, and the wide verandas were embowered. In summer there were many rowboats on the lake, and they lingered more often in the deep shade of the weeping willows fringing the banks. The only blot on the aristocratic landscape was a low brown restaurant kept by a Frenchman, known as "Old Blazes." It was a resort for gay parties that were quite respectable and for others that were not. Behind the public rooms was a row of cubicles patronized by men when on a quiet spree (women, too, it was whispered). There were no cabinet particuliers. Old Blazes had his own ideas of propriety; and no mind to be ousted from Lake Merritt.

Madeleine had found Sally Abbott's society far more endurable, when she paid her round of visits after Masters' departure, than that of the older women with their watchful or anxious eyes, and she had no suspicion that Sally had guessed her secret long since. If love had been her only affliction she would have been grateful for her society and amusing chatter, for they had much in common. But in the circumstances it was unthinkable. Not only was she terrified once more by the prospect of being "cured," but her shattered nerves demanded far more stimulation and tranquilizing than these small daily doses of brandy afforded.

Her will was in no way affected. She controlled even her nerves in Sally's presence, escaped from it twice a day under pretext of taking a nap, and went upstairs immediately after dinner. She had a large room at the back of the house where she could pace up and down unheard.

She pretended to be amiable and resigned, played battledoor and shuttlecock in the hall, or on the lawn when the weather permitted, sang in the evenings with Sally and Harold, and affected not to notice that she was locked in at night. She refused to drive, as she would have found sitting for any length of time unendurable, but she was glad to take long walks even in the rain - and was piloted away from the town and the railroad.

Sally wrote jubilant letters to Dr. Talbot, who thought it best to stay away. The servants were told that Mrs. Talbot was recovering from an illness and suspected nothing.

It lasted two weeks. Sally had inexorably diminished the doses after the seventh day. Madeleine's mind, tormented by her nerves, never ceased for a moment revolving plans for escape.

As they returned from a walk one afternoon they met callers at the door and it was impossible to deny them admittance. Madeleine excused herself and went up to her room wearing her coat and hat instead of handing them to Sally as usual. She put them in her wardrobe and locked the door and hid the key. At dinner it was apparent, however, that Sally had not noticed the omission of this detail in her daily espionage, for the visitors had told her much interesting gossip and she was interested in imparting it. Moreover, her mind was almost at rest regarding her captive.

Madeleine, some time since, had found that the key of another door unlocked her own, and secreted it. She had no money, but she had worn a heavy gold bracelet when her husband and Sally dressed her and they had pinned her collar with a pearl brooch. Sally followed her to her room after she had had time to undress and gave her the nightly draught, but did not linger; she had no mind that her husband should feel neglected and resent this interruption of an extended honeymoon.

Madeleine waited until the house was quiet. Then she went down the heavily carpeted stairs and let herself out by one of the long French windows. She had made her plans and walked swiftly to the restaurant. She knew "Old Blazes," for she had dined at his famous hostelry more than once with her husband or friends.

There was a party in the private restaurant. She walked directly to one of the cubicles and rang for a waiter and told him to send M'sieu to her at once.

"Old Blazes" came immediately, and if she expected him to look astonished she was agreeably disappointed. Nothing astonished him.

She held out her bracelet and brooch. "I want you to lend me some money on these," she said. "My husband will redeem them."

"Very well, madame." (He was far too discreet to recognize her.) "I will bring you the money at once."

"And I wish to buy a quart of Bourbon, which I shall take with me. You may also bring me a glass."

"Very well, madame."

He left the room and returned in a moment with a bottle of Bourbon, from which he had drawn the cork, a glass, and a bottle of Napa Soda. He also handed her two gold pieces. He had been a generous friend to many patrons and had reaped his reward.

"I should advise you to leave by the back entrance," he said. "Shall I have a hack there - in -"

"Send for it at once and I will take it when I am ready. Tell the man to drive on to the boat and to the Occidental Hotel."

"Yes, Madame. Good-night, Madame."

He closed the door. Madeleine left the restaurant three quarters of an hour later.

XXXIV

Colonel Belmont, Alexander Groome, Amos Lawton, Ogden Bascom and several other worthy citizens, were returning from a pleasant supper at Blazes'. They sat for a time in the saloon of the ferry boat El Capitan with the birds of gorgeous plumage they had royally entertained and then went outside to take the air; the ladies preferring to nap.

"Hello! What's that?" exclaimed Groome. "Something's up. Let's investigate."

At the end of the rear deck was a group of men and one or two women. They were crowding one another and those on the edge stood on tiptoe. Belmont was very tall and he could see over their heads without difficulty.

"It's a woman," he announced to his friends. "Drunk - or in a dead faint -"

A man laughed coarsely. "Drunk as they make 'em. No faint about that - Hi! - Quit yer shovin' -"

Belmont scattered the crowd as if they had been children and picked up the woman in his arms.

"My God!" he cried to his staring companions, and as

he faced them he looked about to faint himself. "Do you see who it is? Where can we hide her?"

"Whe-e-ew!" whistled Groome, and for the moment was thankful for his Maria. "What the -"

"I've got my hack on the deck below," said one of the gaping crowd. "She came in it. Better take her right down, sir. I never seen her before but I seen she was a lady and tried to prevent her -"

"Lead the way.... I'll take her home," he said to the others. "And let's keep this dark if we can."

When the hack reached the Occidental Hotel he gave the driver a twenty-dollar gold piece and the man readily promised to "keep his mouth shut." He told the night clerk that Mrs. Talbot had sprained her ankle and fainted, and demanded a pass key if the doctor were out. A bell boy opened the parlor door of the Talbot suite and Colonel Belmont took off Madeleine's hat, placed her on the bed, and then went in search of the doctor.

When Madeleine opened her eyes her husband was sitting beside her. He poured some aromatic spirits of ammonia into a glass of water and she drank it indifferently.

"How did I get here?" she asked.

He told her in the bitterest words he had ever used.

"You are utterly disgraced. Some of those men may hold their tongues but others will not. By this time it is probably all over the Union Club. You are an outcast from this time forth."

"That means nothing to me. And I warned you."

"It is nothing to you that you have disgraced me also, I suppose?"

"No. You made an outcast of Langdon Masters. You wrecked his life and will be the cause of his early death. Meanwhile he is in the gutter. I am glad that I am publicly beside him.... Still, I would have spared you if I could. You are a good man according to your lights. If you had heeded my warning and made no foolish attempts to cure me, no one would have been the wiser."

"Several of the women knew it. And if you had taken advantage of the opportunity given you by Sally I think they would have guarded your secret. You have publicly disgraced them as well as yourself and your husband."

"Well, what shall you do? Throw me into the street? I wish that you would."

"No, I shall try to cure you again."

"And have a wife that your friends will cut dead? You'd be far better off if I *were* dead."

"Perhaps. But I shall do my duty. And if I can cure you I'll sell my practice and go elsewhere. To South America, perhaps."

"Scandal travels. You would never get away from it. Better stay here with your friends, who will not visit my sins on your head. They will never desert you. And you cannot cure me. Did you ever know any one to be cured against his will?"

"I shall lock you in these rooms and you can't drink what you haven't got."

"I've circumvented you before and I shall again."

"Then," he cried violently, "I'll put you in the Home for Inebriates!"

She laughed mockingly. "You'll never do anything of the sort. And I shouldn't care if you did. I should escape."

"Have you no pride left?"

"It is as dead as everything else but this miserable shell. As dead as all that was great in Langdon Masters. Won't you let me die in my own way?"

"I will not."

She sighed and moved her head restlessly on the pillow. "You mean to do what is right, I suppose. But you are cruel, cruel. You condemn me to live in torment."

"I shall give you more for a while than I did before. I was too abrupt. I wouldn't face the whole truth, I suppose."

"I'll kill myself."

"I have no fear of that. You are as superstitious as all

religious women - although much good your religion seems to do you. And you have the same twisted logic as all women, clever as you are. You would drink yourself to death if I would let you, but you'd never commit the overt act. If you are relying on your jewels to bribe the servants with, you will not find them. They are in the safe at the Club. And I shall discontinue your allowance."

"Very well. Please go. I should like to take my bath."

He was obliged to attend an important consultation an hour later, but he did not lock the doors as he had threatened. He wanted as little scandal in the hotel as possible, and he believed her to be helpless without money. The barkeeper was an old friend of his, and when he instructed him to honor no orders from his suite he knew, that the man's promise could be relied on. The chambermaid was dismissed.

As soon as she was alone Madeleine wrote to her father and asked him for a thousand dollars. It was the first time she had asked him for money since her marriage; and he sent it to her with a long kindly letter, warning her against extravagance. She had given no reason for her request, but he inferred that she had been running up bills and was afraid to tell her husband. Was she ill, that she wrote so seldom? He understood that she had quite recovered. But she must remember that he and her mother were old people.

Several days after her return she had sold four new gowns, recently arrived from New York and unworn, to Sibyl Forbes.

XXXV

Ralph Holt ran down the steps of a famous night restaurant in north Montgomery Street on the edge of Chinatown. It was a disreputable place but it had a certain air of brilliancy, although below the sidewalk, and was favored by men that worked late on newspapers, not only for its excellent cuisine but because there was likely to be some garish bit of drama to refresh the jaded mind.

The large room was handsomely furnished with mahogany and lit by three large crystal chandeliers and many side brackets. It was about two thirds full. A band was playing and on a platform a woman in a Spanish costume of sorts was dancing the can-can, to the noisy appreciation of the male guests. Along one side of the room was a bar with a large painting above it of bathing nymphs. The waiters were Chinese.

Holt found an unoccupied table and ordered an oyster stew, then glanced about him for possible centres of interest. There were many women present, gaudily attired, but they were not the elite of the half-world. Neither did the gentlemen who made life gay and carefree for the haughty ladies of the lower ten thousand patronize anything so blatant. They were far too high-toned themselves. Their standards were elevated, all things considered.

But the women of commerce, of whatever status, had no interest for young Holt save as possible heroines of living drama. He had a lively news sense, and although an editor, and of a highly respectable sheet at that, he could become as keen on the track of a "story" as if he were still a reporter.

But although the night birds were eating little and drinking a great deal, at this hour of two in the morning, the only excitement was the marvellous high kicking of the black-eyed scantily clad young woman on the stage and the ribald applause of her admirers.

His eye was arrested by the slender back of a woman who sat at a table alone drinking champagne. She was so simply dressed that she was far more noticeable than if she had crowned herself with jewels. His lunch arrived at the moment, and it was not until he had satisfied his usual morning appetite that he remembered the woman and glanced her way again. Two men were sitting at her table, apparently endeavoring to engage her in conversation. They belonged to the type loosely known as men about town, of no definite position, but with money to spend and a turn for adventure.

It was equally apparent that they received no response to their amiable overtures, for they shrugged their shoulders in a moment, laughed, and went elsewhere. More than one woman sat alone and these were amenable enough. They came for no other purpose.

Holt paid his account and strolled over to the table. When he took one of the chairs he was shocked but not particularly surprised to see that the woman was Mrs. Talbot. The town had rung with her story all winter, and he had heard several months since that she had obtained money in some way and left her husband. The report was that Dr. Talbot had traced her to lodgings on the Plaza, but she had not only refused to return to him but to tell him where she had obtained her funds. She had informed him that she had sufficient money to keep her "long enough," but the doctor had his misgivings and directed his lawyers to pay the rent of the room and make an arrangement with a neighboring restaurant to send in her meals. Then he had gone off on a sea voyage. Holt had seen him driving his double team the day before, evidently on a round of visits. The sea, apparently, had done him little good. Nothing but age, no doubt, would shatter that superb constitution, but he had lost his ruddy color and his face was drawn and lined.

Madeleine had not raised her eyes. She looked like an effigy of well-bred contempt, and Holt did not wonder that she suffered briefly from the attentions of predatory males in search of amusement. Moreover, she was very thin, and the sirens of that day were voluptuous. They fed on cream and sweets until the proper curves of bust and hips were achieved, and those that appeared in the wrong place were held flat with a broad "wooden whalebone."

Holt was surprised to find her so little changed. It was evident she was one of those drinkers whom liquor made pallid not red; her skin was still smooth and her face had not lost its fine oval. But it was only a matter of time!

"Mrs. Talbot."

She raised her eyes with a faint start and with an expression of haughty disdain. But as she recognized him the expression faded and she regarded him sadly.

"You see," she said.

"It's a crime, you know."

"Have you any news of him?"

"Nothing new. It takes time to kill a man like that."

"I hope he is more fortunate than I am! It hasn't the effect that it did. It keeps my nerves sodden, but my brain is horribly clear. I no longer forget! And death is a long time coming. I am tired always, but I don't break."

"You shouldn't come to such places as this. If a man was drunk enough you couldn't discourage him."

"Oh, I have been spoken to in places like this and on the street by men in every stage of intoxication and by men who were quite sober. But I am able to take care of myself. This sort of man - the only sort I meet now - likes gay clothes and gay women."

"All the same it's not safe. Do you only go out at night?"

"Yes - I - I sleep in the daytime."

"Look here - I have a plan - I won't tell you what it is now – but meanwhile I wish you would promise me that you will not go out alone - to hells of this sort - again. I can make an arrangement for a while at the office to get off earlier, and I'll take you wherever you want to go. Is it a bargain?"

"Very well," she said indifferently. Then she smiled for the first time, and her face looked sweet and almost girlish once more. "You are very kind. Why do you take so much interest? I am only one more derelict. You must have seen many."

"Well, I'm just built that way. I took a shine to you the day in that old ark we ambled about in, and then I'm as fond of Masters as ever. D'you see? Now, let's get out of this. I'm going to see you home."

"Home!"

"Well, I'm glad the word gives you a shock, anyway. It's where you ought to be."

They left the restaurant and although, when they reached the sidewalk, she took his arm, he noticed that she did not stagger.

They walked up the hill past the north side of the Plaza. The gambling houses of the fifties and early sixties had moved elsewhere, and although there were low-browed shops on the east side with flaring gas jets before them even at this hour, the other three sides, devoted to offices and rooming-houses, were respectable. There were a few drunken sailors on the grass, who had wandered too far from Barbary Coast, but they were asleep.

"I never am molested here," she said. "I don't think I have ever met any one. Sometimes I have stood in the shadow up there and looked down Dupont Street. What a sight! Respectable Montgomery Street is never so crowded at four in the afternoon. And the women! Sometimes I have envied them, for life has never meant anything to them but just that. I never saw one of those painted harlots who looked as if she had even the remnants of a mind."

"Well, for heaven's sake keep your distance from Dupont Street. If some drunken brute caught you lurking in the shadows it might appeal to his sense of humor to toss you on his shoulder and run the length of the street with you - possibly fling you through one of the windows of those awful cottages into some harlot's lap, if she happened to be soliciting at the moment. Then she'd scratch your eyes out.... You know a lot about taking care of yourself," he fumed.

"Oh, I never go there any more," she said indifferently. "I'm tired of it."

"I can understand you leaving your husband and wishing to live alone - natural enough! - but what I cannot understand is that you, the quintessence of delicate breeding, should walk the streets at night and sit in dives. I wonder you can stand being in the room with such women, to say nothing of the men."

"It has been my hope to forget all I represented before, and danger means nothing to me. Moreover, there are other reasons. I must have exercise and air. I do not care to risk meeting any of my old friends. I must get away from myself - from solitude - during some part of the twenty-four hours. And - well - the die was cast. I was publicly disgraced. It doesn't matter what I do now, and when I sit in that sort of place I can imagine that he is in similar ones on the other side of the continent. I told you that I intended to be no better than he - and of course as I am a woman I am worse."

"I suppose you would not be half so charming if you were not so completely feminine. But just how many of these night hells have you been to?"

"I can't tell. I've been to far worse dives than that. I've even been in saloons over on Barbary Coast. But although I've been hurt accidentally several times in scuffles, and a bullet nearly hit me once, I seem to bear a charmed life. I suppose those do that want to die. And although they treat me with no respect they seem to regard me as a harmless lunatic, and - and - I take very little when I am out. I have just enough pride left not to care to be taken to the calaboose by a policeman."

"Good God! How can you even talk of such things? Some day you will regret all this horribly."

"I'll never regret anything except that I was born."

"Well, here we are. I'll not take you up to your rooms. Don't give them a chance at that sort of scandal whatever you do. It's lucky for you that alcohol doesn't send you along a still livelier road to perdition. It does most women."

"I see him every moment. Even if I did not, I do not think - well, of course if things were different I should not be an outcast of any sort. And don't imagine that my refinement suffers in these new contacts. The underworld interests me; I had never even tried to imagine it before. I am permitted to remain aloof and a spectator. At times it is all as unreal as I seem to myself, sitting there. But I never feel so close to vice as to complete honesty. I have often had glimpses of blacker sins in Society."

"Well, I'm glad it's no worse. To tell you the truth, I've avoided looking you up, for I didn't know - well, I didn't want to see you again if you were too different. Good-night. I'll meet you at this door tonight at twelve sharp."

XXXVI

There were doctors' offices on the first floor and Madeleine climbed wearily the two flights to her room. Her muscles felt as tired as her spirit, but she had an odd fancy that her skeleton was of fine flexible steel and not only indestructible but tenacious and dominant. It defied the worst she could do to organs and soul.

She unlocked her door and lit the gas jet. It was a decent room, large, with the bed in an alcove, and little uglier than those grim double parlors of her past that she had graced so often. But her own rooms at the hotel had been beautiful and luxurious. They had sheltered and pampered her body for five years, and her father's house was a stately mansion, refurnished, with the exception of old colonial pieces, after the grand tour in Europe. This room, although clean and sufficiently equipped, was sordid and commonplace, and the bed was as hard as the horsehair furniture. Her body as well as her aesthetic sense had rebelled more than once.

But she would never return; although she guessed that the complete dissociation from her old life and its tragic reminders had more than a little to do with the loathing for drink that had gradually possessed her. She had not admitted it to Holt, but it required a supreme effort of will to take a glass of hot whiskey and water at night, the taste disguised as much as possible by lime juice, and another in the daytime. She had no desire to reform! And she longed passionately to drown not only her heart but her pride. Now that her system was refusing its demoralizing drug she felt that horror of her descent only possible to a woman who has inherited and practised all the refinements of civilization. She longed to return to those first months of degraded oblivion, and could not!

The champagne or brandy she was forced to order in the dives she haunted, in order to secure a table, merely gave her tone for the moment.

Her nerves were less affected than her spirits. She had hours of such black depression that only the faint glimmering star of religion kept her from suicide. She had longer seasons for thought on Masters and his ruin - and of the hours they had spent together. One night she went out to Dolores and sat in the dark little church until dawn. She had nothing of the saint in her and felt no impulse to emulate Concha Arguello, who had become the first nun in California; moreover, Razanov had died an honorable death through no fault of his or his Concha's. She and Langdon Masters were lost souls and must expiate their sins in the eyes of the world that heaped on their heads its pitiless scorn.

Madeleine threw off her hat and dropped into the armchair, oblivious of its bumps. She began to cry quietly with none of her former hysteria. Holt was nearer to Masters than any one she knew, and she was grateful that he had not seen her in her hours of supreme degradation. If he ever saw Masters again he would tell him of her downfall, of course - and the reason for it; but at least he could paint no horrible concrete picture. For the first time she felt thankful that she had not sunk lower; been compelled, indeed, against her will, to retrace her steps. She even regretted the hideous episode of the ferry boat, although she had welcomed the exposure at the time. Her pride was lifting its battered head, and although she felt no remorse, and was without hope, and her unclouded consciousness foreshadowed long years of spiritual torment and longing with not a diversion to lighten the gloom, she possessed herself more nearly that night than since Holt had given her what she had believed to be her death blow.

If she could only die. But death was no friend of hers.

XXXVII

That afternoon Holt called on Dr. Talbot in his office. Half an hour later, looking flushed and angry, he strolled frowning down Bush street, then turned abruptly and walked in the direction of South Park. He did not know Mrs. McLane but he believed she would see him.

He called at midnight - and on many succeeding nights - for Madeleine and took her to several of the dives that seemed to afford her amusement. He noticed that she drank little, and had a glimmering of the truth. Newspaper men have several extra senses. It was also apparent that the life she had led had not made her callous. As he insisted upon "treating" her she would have none of champagne but ordered ponies of brandy.

Now that she had a cavalier she was stared at more than formerly, and there was some audible ribald comment which Holt did his best to ignore; but as time wore on those bent on hilarity or stupor ceased to notice two people uninterestingly sober.

Holt talked of Masters constantly, relating every incident of his sojourn in San Francisco he could recall, and of his past that had come to his knowledge; expatiating bitterly upon his wasted gifts and blasted life. The more Madeleine winced the further he drove in the knife.

One night they were sitting on a balcony in Chinatown. In the restaurant behind them a banquet was being given by a party of Chinese merchants, and Holt had thought the scene might amuse her. The round table was covered with dishes no larger than those played with in childhood and the portions were as minute. The sleek merchants wore gorgeously embroidered costumes, and behind them were women of their own race, dressed plainly in the national garb, their stiff oiled hair stuck with long pins lobed with glass. They were evidently an orchestra, for they sang, or rather chanted, in high monotonous voices, as mournful as their gray expressionless faces. In two recesses, extended on teakwood couches, were Chinamen presumably of the same class as the diners, but wearing their daily blue silk unadorned and leisurely smoking the opium pipe. The room was heavily gilded and decorated and on the third floor as befitted its rank. Chinamen of humbler status dined on the floor below, and the ground restaurant accommodated the coolies.

On the little balcony, their chairs wedged between large vases of growing plants, Madeleine could watch the function without attracting attention; or lean over the railing and look down upon the narrow street hung with gay paper lanterns above the open doors of shops that flaunted the wares of the Orient under strange gilt signs. There were many little balconies high above the street and they were as brilliantly lit as for a festival. From several came the sound of raucous instrumental music or that same thin chant as of lost souls wandering in outer darkness. The street was thronged with Chinamen of the lower caste in dark blue cotton smocks, pendent pigtails, and round coolie hats.

It was eight o'clock, but it was Holt's "night off" and as he had told her that morning he could get a pass for the dinner, and that it was time she "changed her bill," she had risen early and met him at her door.

It was apparent that she took a lively interest in this bit of Shanghai but a step out of the Occident, for her face had lost its heavy brooding and she asked him many questions. It was an hour before Masters' name was mentioned, and then she said abruptly:

"You tell me much of his life out here and before he came, but you hardly ever say anything about the present."

"That sort of life is much of a muchness."

"How do you hear?"

"One of the *Bulletin* men - Tom Lacey - went East just after Masters did. He is on the *Times*. Several of us correspond with him."

"Has - has he ever been - literally, I mean - in the gutter?"

"Probably. He was in a hospital for a time and when he came out several of his friends tried to buck him up. But it was no use. He did work on one of the newspapers - the *Tribune*, I believe - about half sober until he had paid his hospital bill with something to spare. Then he went to work in the same old steady painstaking way to drink himself to death."

"Wh - why did he go to the hospital? Was he very ill?"

"Busted the crust of a policeman and got his own busted at the same time."

"How is it you spared me this before?"

He pretended not to see her tears, or her working hands.

"Didn't want to give you too heavy doses at once, but you are so much stronger that I chanced it. He's been in more than one spectacular affair. One night, in front of the City Prison, he tossed the driver off a van as if the man had been a dead leaf, and before the guard had time to jump to his seat he was on the box and had lashed the horses. He drove like mad all over New York for hours, the prisoners inside yelling and cursing at the top of their lungs. They thought it was a new and devilishly ingenious mode of punishment. When the horses dropped he left the van where it stood and went home. There was a frightful row over the affair. Masters was arrested, of course, but bailed out. He has friends still and some of them are influential. The trial was postponed a few times and then dropped. His rows are too numerous to mention. When he was here and sober he betrayed anger only in his eyes, which looked like steel blades run through fire, and with the most caustic tongue ever put in a man's head. But when he's in certain stages of insobriety his fighting instincts appear to take their own sweet way. At other times, Lacey writes, he is as interesting as ever and men sit round eagerly and listen to him talk. At others he simply disappears. Did I tell you he had come into a little money - just recently?"

"No, you did not. Why doesn't he start a newspaper?"

"He's probably forgotten he ever wanted one - no, I don't fancy he ever forgets anything. Only death will destroy that brain no matter how he may obfuscate it. And I guess there are times when he can't, poor devil. But he couldn't start a newspaper on what he's got. It's just enough to buy him all he wants without the necessity for work."

"How did he get it?"

"His elder brother - only remaining member of the immediate family - died and left him the old plantation in Virgina - what there is left of it; and a small income from two or three old houses in Richmond. Masters told me once that when the war left them high and dry he agreed to waive his share in the estate provided his brother would take care of his mother and the old place. The estate comes to him now, but in trust. At his death, without legal heir, it goes to a cousin."

"Oh, take me home, please. I can't stand those wailing women any longer."

XXXVIII

A month later there was a tap on Madeleine's door. She rose earlier these days and opened it at once, assuming that it was a message from Holt. But Mr. McLane stood there.

"How are you, Madeleine? May I come in?" He shook her half-extended hand as if he were paying her an afternoon call at the Occidental Hotel, and sat down on the horsehair sofa with a genial smile; placing his high silk hat and gold-headed cane beside him.

"Glad to see you looking so well. I've wanted to call for a long time, but as you dropped us all like so many hot potatoes, I hesitated, and was delighted today when Howard gave me an excuse."

"Howard?"

"Yes, he wants you to go back to him."

"That I'll never do."

"Don't be hasty. He is willing to forget everything - he asked me to make you understand that he would never mention the subject. He will also put your share of your father's estate unreservedly in your hands as soon as the usual legal delays are over. You knew that your father was dead, did you not? And your mother also?"

"Oh yes, I knew. It didn't seem to make any difference. I knew I never should see them again anyhow."

"Howard was appointed trustee of your inheritance, but as I said, he does not mean to take advantage of the fact. I am informed, by the way, that your brother never told your parents that you had left Howard. He knew nothing beyond the fact, of course."

"Well, I am glad of that."

She had no intention of shedding any tears before Mr. McLane. Let him think her callous if he must.

"About Howard?"

"I'll never go back to him. I never want to see him again."

"Not if he would take you to Europe to live? There is an opening for an American doctor in Paris."

"I never want to see him again. I know he is a good man but I hate him. And if I did go back it would be worse. You may tell him that."

"Is your decision irrevocable?"

"Yes, it is."

"Then I must tell you that if there is no prospect of your return he will divorce you."

"Divorced - I divorced?" Her eyes expanded with

horrified astonishment. But only for a moment. She threw back her head and laughed. "That was funny, wasn't it? Well, let him do as he thinks best. And he may be happy once more if I am out of his life altogether. He won't have much trouble getting a divorce!"

"He will obtain it on the ground of desertion."

"Oh! Well, he was always a very good man. Poor Howard! I hope he'll marry again and be happy."

"Better think it over. I - by the way - I'm not sure the women wouldn't come round in time; particularly if you lived abroad for a few years."

She curled her lip. "And I should have my precious position in Society again! How much do you suppose that means to me? Have the fatted calf killed and coals of fire poured on my humbled head! Do you think I have no pride?"

"You appear to have regained it. I wish you could regain the rest and be the radiant creature you were when you came to us. God! What a lovely stunning creature you were! It hurts me like the devil, I can tell you. And it's hurt the women too. They were fond of you. Do you know that Sally is dead?"

"Yes. She had everything to live for and she died. Life seems to amuse herself with us."

"She's a damned old hag." He rose and took up his hat and cane. "Well, I'll wait a week, and then if you don't relent the proceedings will begin. I shan't get the divorce. Not my line. But he asked me to talk to you and I was glad to come. Good-by."

She smiled as she shook hands with him. As he opened the door he turned to her again.

"That young Holt is a good fellow and has a head on his shoulders. Better be guided by him if he offers you any advice."

XXXIX

Almost insensibly and without comment Madeleine
fell into the habit of sleeping at night and going abroad
with Holt in the daytime. Nor did he take her to any
more dives. They went across the Bay, either to
Oakland or Sausalito, and took long walks, dining at
some inn where they were sure to meet no one they
knew. She had asked him to buy her books, as she did
not care to venture either into the bookstores or the
Mercantile Library. She now had a part of her new
income to spend as she chose, and moved into more
comfortable rooms, although far from the fashionable
quarter. She was restless and often very nervous but
Holt knew that she drank no longer. There had been
another revolution of the wheel: she would have a
large income, freedom impended, the future was hers
to dispose of at will. Her health was excellent; she had
regained her old proud bearing.

"What are you going to do with it?" he asked her
abruptly one evening. They were sitting in the arbor of
a restaurant on the water front at Sausalito and had just
finished dinner. The steep promontory rose behind
them a wild forest of oak and pine, madrona and
chaparral. Across the sparkling dark green water San
Francisco looked a pale blue in the twilight and there
was a banner of soft pink above her. Lights were
appearing on the military islands, the ferry boats, and

yachts. "You will be free in about a month now. Have you made any plans? You will not stay here, of course."

"Stay here! I shall leave the day the decree is granted, and I'll never see California again as long as I live."

"But where shall you go?"

"Oh - it would be interesting to live in Europe."

"Whether you have admitted it to yourself or not you have not the remotest idea of going to Europe."

"Oh?"

"You are going to Langdon Masters. Nothing in the world could keep you away from him - or should."

"I wish women smoked. You look so placid. And I am glad you smoke cigarettes."

"Why not try one?"

"Oh, no!" She looked scandalized. "I never did that - before. The other was for a purpose, not because I liked it."

"I am used to your line of ratiocination. But you haven't answered my question."

"Did you ask one?"

"In the form of an assertion, yes."

"You know - the Church forbids marriage after divorce."

"Look here, Madeleine!" Holt brought his fist down on the table with such violence that she half started to her feet. "Do you mean to tell me you are going to let any more damn foolishness wreck your life a second time?"

"You must not speak of the Church in that way."

"Let that pass. I am not going to argue with you. You've argued it all out with yourself unless I'm much mistaken. Are you going to let Masters kill himself when you can save him? Are you going to condemn yourself to a miserably solitary, wandering, aimless life, in which you are no good to yourself, your Church, or any one on earth - and with a crime on your soul?"

I - I - haven't admitted to myself what I shall do. It has seemed to me that when I am free I shall simply go -"

"And straight to Masters. As well for a needle to try to run away from a magnet."

"Oh, I wonder! I wonder!" But she did not look distressed. Her face was transfigured as if she saw a vision. But it fell in a moment, that inner glowing lamp extinguished.

"He may no longer want me. He may have forgotten me. Or if he remembers it must only be to remind himself that I have ruined his life. He may hate me."

"That is likely! If he hated you he'd have pulled up

long ago. He knows he still has it in him to make a name for himself, whether he owns a newspaper or not. If he's gone on making a fool of himself it's because his longing for you is insupportable; he can forget you in no other way."

"Can men really love like that?" The inner lamp glowed again.

"A few. Not many, perhaps. Langdon's one of them. Case of a rare whole being chopped in two by fate and both halves bleeding to death without the other. There are a few immortal love affairs in the world's history, and that's just what makes 'em immortal."

She did not answer, but sat staring at the rosy peaceful light above the fiery city that had burnt out so many lives. Then her face changed suddenly. It was set and determined, almost hard. He thought she looked like a beautiful Medusa.

"Yes," she said. "I am going to him. I suppose I have known it all along. At all events I know it now."

"And what is your plan?"

"I have had no time to make one yet."

"Will you listen to mine?"

"Do not I always listen to you with the greatest respect?" She was the charming woman again. "Mr. McLane told me that I was to follow your advice - I have an idea you have engineered this whole affair! - But if he hadn't - well, I have every reason to be humbly grateful to you. If this terrible tangle ever unravels I shall owe it to you."

"Then listen to me now. What I said - that his actions prove that he cares for you as much as ever - is true. But - you might come upon him in a condition where he would not recognize you, or was morose from too much drink or too little; and for the moment he would hate you, either because you reminded him too forcibly of what he had been and was, or because it degraded him further to be seen by you in such a state. He could make himself excessively disagreeable sober. Drunk, panic stricken, reckless, I should think he might achieve a masterpiece in that line that would make you feel like ten cents.... This is my plan. I'll go on at once and prepare him. Get him down to his home in Virginia on one pretence or another, sober him up by degrees, and then tell him all you have been through for his sake, and that as soon as you are free you will come to him. He'll be a little more like himself by that time and can stand having you look at him.... It'll be no easy task at first; and I'll have to taper him off to prevent any blow to his heart. There may be relapses, and the whole thing to do over; but I shall use the talisman of your name as soon as he is in a condition to understand, and shall succeed in the end. Once let the idea take hold of him that he can have you at last and it is only a question of time."

She made no reply for a moment. She sat with her eyes on his as he spoke. At first they had opened widely, melted and flashed. But they narrowed slowly. As he finished she turned her profile toward him and he had never seen a cameo look harder.

"That would be an easy way out," she said. "But it does not appeal to me. Nothing easy appeals to me these days. I'll fight my own battles and overcome my own obstacles. Besides, he's mine. He shall owe nothing to any one but to me. I'll find him and cure him myself."

"But you'll have a hard time finding him. He disappears for weeks at a time. Even Tom Lacey might not be able to help you."

"I'll find him."

"You may have to haunt the most abominable places."

"You seem to forget that I have haunted a good many abominable places. And if they are good enough for him they are good enough for me."

"New York has the worst set of roughs in the world. Our hoodlums are lambs beside them."

"I have no fear of anything but not finding him in time."

"But that is not the worst. You should not see him in that state. You might find him literally in the gutter. He might be a sight you never could forget. No matter what you made of him you never could obliterate such a hideous memory. And he might say things to you that your outraged pride would never forgive."

"I can forget anything I choose. Nor could anything he said, nor anything he may have become, horrify me. Don't you think I have pictured all that? I think of him every moment and I am not a coward. I have imagined things that may be worse than the reality."

"Hardly. But there is another danger. You might

kidnap him and get him sobered up, only to lose him again. He might be so overcome with shame that he would cut loose and hide where you would never find him. Remember, his pride was as great as yours."

"I'd track him to the ends of the earth. He's mine and I'll have him."

Holt stared at her for a moment in perplexity, then laughed. "You are a liberal education, Madeleine. Just as I think I really know you at last you break out in a new place. Masters will have an interesting life. You must be a sort of continued-in-our-next story for any one who has the right to love and live with you. But for any one else who has loved you it must be death and damnation."

She stole a glance at him, wondering if he loved her. If he did he had never made a sign, and at the moment he seemed to be appraising her with his sharp cool blue eyes.

"I was thinking of the doctor," he said calmly. "Although, of course, there must have been a good many in a more or less idiotic state over the reigning toast."

"The reigning toast!... Well, I'll never be that again. But it won't matter if - when - You are to promise me you will not write to him!"

"Oh, yes, I promise." Holt had been rapidly formulating his own plans. "But you'll let me give you a letter to Lacey? It's a wild goose chase but a little advice might help."

"I should have asked you for a line to Mr. Lacey. I don't wish to waste time if I can help it."

He rose. "Well, there's a pile of blank paper and a soft pencil waiting for me. I've an editorial to write on the low-lived politics of San Francisco, and another on the increasing number of murders in our fair city. Look at the fog sailing in through the Golden Gate, pushing itself along like the prow of a ship. You'll never see anything as beautiful as California again. But I suppose that worries you a lot."

She smiled, a little mysterious smile, but she did not reply, and they walked down to the ferry slip in silence.

XL

Madeline went directly from the train to Printing House Square and had a long talk with "Tom" Lacey. He had been advised of her coming and her quest and had already made a search for Masters, but without result. This he had no intention of imparting, however, but told her a carefully prepared story.

Masters had been writing regularly for some time and it was generally believed among his friends that he had pulled up in a measure, but where he was hiding himself no one knew. Cheques and suggestions were sent to the Post Office, but he had no box, nor did he call for his mail in person.

He appeared no more at the restaurants in Nassau or Fulton Streets, or in Park Row, and it would be idle to look for him up town. It was apparent that he wished to avoid his friends, and to do this effectually he had probably hidden himself in one of the rabbit warrens of Nassau Street, where the King of England or the Czar of all the Russias might hide for a lifetime and never be found. But Masters could be "located," no doubt of that. "It only needs patience and alertness," said Lacey, looking straight into Madeleine's vigilant eyes. "I have a friend on the police force down there who will spot him before long and send for me hot-foot."

It was Lacey's intention to sublet a small office in one of the swarming buildings, put a cot in it and a cooking stove, and transfer Masters to it as soon as he was found. He knew what some of Masters' haunts were and had no intention that this delicate proud woman should see him in any of them.

When she told him that she should never leave Masters again after his whereabouts had been discovered, he warned her not to take rooms in a hotel. There would be unpleasant espionage, possibly newspaper scandal. There was nothing for it but Bleecker Street. It was outwardly quiet, the rooms were large and comfortable in many of those once-fashionable houses, and it was the one street in New York where no questions were asked and no curiosity felt. It was no place for her, of course - but under the circumstances - if she persisted in her idea of keeping Masters with her until his complete recovery -

"My neighbors will not worry me," she said, smiling for the first time. "It seems to be just the place. I already feel bewildered in this great rushing noisy city. I have lived in a small city for so long that I had almost forgotten there were great ones; and I should not know what to do without your advice. I am very grateful."

"Glad to do anything I can. When Holt wrote me you were coming and there was a chance to pull Masters out of the - put him on his legs again, I went right up in the air. You may count on me. Always glad to do anything I can for a lady, too. I used to see you at the theatre and driving, Mrs. Talbot, and wished I were one of the bloods. Seems like a fairy tale to be able to help you now."

He had red hair and slate-colored eyes, a snub nose and many freckles, but she thought him quite beautiful; he was her only friend in this terrifying city, and there was no doubt she could count on him.

"How shall I go about finding a lodging in Bleecker Street?" she asked. "I stayed at the Fifth Avenue Hotel when I visited New York with my mother, and as I know nothing of the other hotels, I left my luggage at the depot until I should have seen you. I didn't dare go where I might run into any one. Californians are beginning to visit New York. Moreover, my brother and his family live here and I particularly wish to avoid them."

"A theatrical troupe is just leaving town - so there should be several empty rooms. A good many of them hang out there when in New York. There is one thing in your favor. Your - pardon me - beauty won't be so conspicuous in Bleecker Street as it would be in hotels. It isn't only actresses that lodge there, but - well - those ladies so richly dowered by nature they command the longest pocketbooks, and the owners thereof sometimes have a pew in Trinity Church and a seat on the Stock Exchange. The great world averts its eyes from Bleecker Street, and you will be as safe in there as the most respectable sinner. Nor will you be annoyed by rowdyism in the street, although you may hear echoes of high old times going on in some of the houses patronized by artists and students - it's a sort of Latin Quarter, too. Little of everything, in fact. Now, come along. We'll take a hack, get your luggage, and fix you up."

"And you'll vow -"

"To send for you the moment Masters is located? Just rely on Tom Lacey."

XLI

Madeline took two floors of a large brown stone house in Bleecker Street, and the accommodating landlady found a colored wench to keep her rooms in order and cook her meals. A room at the back and facing the south was fitted up for Masters. It was a masculine-looking room with its solid mahogany furniture, and as his books were stored in the cellar of the Times Building she had shelves built to the ceiling on the west wall. Lacey obtained an order for the books without difficulty, and Madeleine disposed of several of her long evenings filling the shelves. When she had finished, one side of the large room at least looked exactly like his parlor in the Occidental Hotel. She also hung the windows with green curtains and draped the mantelpiece with the same material. Green had been his favorite color.

She had rebelled at giving up her original purpose of making a personal search for Masters, but one look at New York had convinced her that if Lacey would not help her she must employ a detective. Nevertheless, she went every mid-day to one or other of the restaurants below Chambers Street; and, although nothing had ever terrified her so much, she ventured into Nassau Street at least once a day and struggled through it, peering into every face.

Nassau Street was only ten blocks long and very narrow, but it would seem as if, during the hours of business, a cyclone gathered all the men in New York and hurled them in compact masses down its length until they were met by another cyclone that drove them back again. They filled the street as well as the narrow sidewalks, they poured out of the doorways as if impelled from behind, and Madeleine wondered they did not jump from the windows. No one sauntered, all rushed along with tense faces; there were many collisions and no one paused to apologize, nor did any one seem to expect it. There were hundreds, possibly thousands, of offices in those buildings high for their day, and every profession, every business, every known or unique occupation, was represented. There were banks and newspaper buildings, hotels, restaurants, auction rooms, the Treasury and the old Dutch Church that had been turned into the General Post Office. There were shops containing everything likely to appeal to men, although one wondered when they found time for anything so frivolous as shopping; second-hand book stores, and street hawkers without number.

In addition to the thousands of men who seemed to be hurrying to and from some business of vital import, there were the hundred thousand or more who surged through that narrow thoroughfare every day for their mail. The old church looked like a besieged fortress and Madeleine marvelled that it did not collapse. She was thankful that she was never obliged to enter it. Holt and her lawyer had been instructed to send their letters to Lacey's care, and Lacey when obliged to communicate with her, either called or sent his note by a messenger.

Madeleine was so hustled, stepped on, whirled about, that she finally made friends with an old man who kept one of the secondhand shops, and, comparatively safe, used the doorway as her watch tower.

One day she thought she saw Masters and darted out into the street. There she fought her way in the wake of a tall stooping man with black hair as mercilessly as if she were some frantic woman who had risked her all on the Stock Exchange. He entered the door of one of the tall buildings, and when she reached it she heard the sound of footsteps rapidly mounting.

She followed as rapidly. The footsteps ceased. When she arrived at the fourth floor she knocked on every door in turn. It was evidently a building that housed men of the dingiest social status. Every man who answered her peremptory summons looked like a derelict. These were mere semblances of offices, with unmade beds, sometimes on the floor. In some were dreary looking women, partners, no doubt, of these forlorn men, whose like she sometimes saw down in the street. But her breathless search was fruitless. She knew that one of the men who grudgingly opened his door - looking as if he expected the police - was the man she had followed, and she was grateful that it was not Masters.

She went slowly down the rickety staircase feeling as if she should sink at every step. It had been her first ray of hope in two weeks and she felt faint and sick under the reaction.

She found a coupe in Broadway and was driven to her lodgings. The maid was waiting for her in the doorway, evidently perturbed.

Gertrude Atherton

"There's a strange gentleman upstairs in the parlor, ma'am," she said. "Not Mr. Lacey. I didn't want to let him in but he would. He said -"

She thrust the girl aside and ran up the steps. But when she burst into the parlor the man waiting for her was Ralph Holt.

She dropped into a chair and began to cry hysterically. He had dealt with her in that state before, and Amanda had lived in Bleecker Street for many years. She was growing bored with the excessive respectability of her place, and was delighted to find that her mistress was human. Cold water, sal volatile, and hartshorn soon restored Madeleine's composure. She handed her hat to the woman and was alone with Holt.

"I thought - perhaps you understand -"

"I understand, all right. I hope you are not angry with me for following you."

"I am only too glad to see you. I never knew a city could be so big and heartless. I have felt like a leaf tossed about in a perpetual cold wind. When did you arrive?"

"The day after you did."

"What? And you - you - have been looking for him?"

"That is what I came for - partly. Yes, Lacey and I have combed the town."

Madeleine sprang to her feet. "You've found him! I know it! Why don't you say so?"

"Well, we know where he is. But it's no place for you."

"Take me at once. I don't care what it is."

"But I do. So does Lacey. His plan was to shanghai him and sober him up. But - well - it is your right to say whether he shall do that or not. You wanted to find him yourself. But Five Points is no place for you, and I want your permission to carry out Lacey's program."

"What is Five Points?"

"The worst sink in New York. Just imagine the Barbary Coast of San Francisco multiplied by two thousand. There is said to be nothing worse in London or Paris."

"If you and Mr. Lacey do not take me there I shall go alone."

"Be reasonable."

"My reason works quite as clearly as if my heart were chloroformed. Langdon will know, when I track him to a place like that, what he means to me."

"He probably will be in no condition to recognize you."

"I'll make him recognize me. Or if I cannot you may use your force then, but he shall know later that I went there for him. Have you seen him?"

Holt moved uneasily and looked away. "Yes, I have seen him."

"You need not be so distressed. I shall not care what he looks like. I shall see *him* inside. Did you speak to him?"

"He either did not recognize me or pretended not to."

"Well, we go now."

"Won't you think it over?"

"I prefer your escort to that of a policeman. I shall not be so foolish as to go alone."

"Then we'll come for you at about eleven tonight. It would be useless to go look for him now. People who lead that sort of life sleep in the day time. I have not the faintest idea where he lives."

"Very well, I shall have to wait, I suppose."

Holt rose. "Lacey and I will come for you, and we'll bring with us two of the biggest detectives we can find. It's no joke taking a woman - a woman like you - Good God! - into a sewer like that. Even Lacey and I got into trouble twice, but we could take care of ourselves. Better dine with me at Delmonico's and forget things for a while."

"I could not eat, nor sit still. Nor do I wish to run the risk of meeting my brother; or any one else I know. Come for me promptly at eleven or you will not find me here."

XLII

Langdon Masters awoke from a sleep that had lasted all day and glowered out upon the room he occupied in Baxter Street. It was as wretched as all tenements in the Five Points, but it had the distinguishing mark of neatness. Drunk as he might be, the drab who lived with him knew that he would detect dirt and disorder, and that her slender hold on his tolerance would be forfeited at once. There were too many of her sort in the Five Points eager for the position of mistress to this man who treated them as a sultan might treat the meanest of his concubines, rarely throwing them a word, and alternately indulgent and brutal. They regarded him with awe, even forgetting to drink when, in certain stages of his cups, he entertained by the hour in one or other of the groggeries a circle of the most abandoned characters in New York - thieves, cracks-men, murderers actual or potential, "shoulder-hitters," sailors who came ashore to drink the fieriest rum they could find, prostitutes, dead-beats, degenerates, derelicts - with a flow of talk that was like the flashing of jewels in the gutter. He related the most stupendous adventures that had ever befallen a mortal. If any one of his audience had heard of Munchausen he would have dismissed him as a poor imitation of this man who would seem to have dropped down into their filthy and lawless quarter from a sphere where things happened unknown to men on this planet. They dimly recognized that he was a fallen gentleman, for at long intervals good churchmen from the foreign territory of Broadway or Fifth Avenue came to remonstrate and plead. They never came a second time and they usually spent the following week in bed.

But Masters was democratic enough in manner; it was evident that he regarded himself as no better than the worst, and nothing appeared to be further from his mind than reform of them or himself. He had now been with them for six months and came and went as he pleased. In the beginning his indestructible air of superiority had subtly irritated them in spite of his immediate acceptance of their standards, and there had been two attempts to trounce him. But he was apparently made of steel rope, he knew every trick of their none too subtle "game," and he had knocked out his assailants and won the final respect of Five Points.

And if he was finical about his room he took care to be no neater in his dress than his associates. Although he had his hair cut and his face shaved he wore old and rough clothes and a gray flannel shirt.

Masters, after his drab had given him a cup of strong coffee and a rasher, followed by a glass of rum, lost the horrid sensations incident upon the waking moment and looked forward to the night with a sardonic but not discontented grin. He knew that he had reached the lowest depths, and if his tough frame refused to succumb to the vilest liquor he could pour into it, he would probably be killed in some general shooting fray, or by one of the women he infatuated and cast aside when another took his drunken but ever ironic fancy. Only a week since the cyprian at present engaged in washing his dishes had been nearly demolished by the damsel she had superseded. She still wore a livid mark on her cheek and a plaster on her head whence a handful of hair had been removed by the roots. He had stood aloof during the fracas in the dirty garish dance house under the sidewalk, laughing consumedly; and had awakened the next night to find the victor mending her tattered finery. She made him an excellent cup of coffee, and he had told her curtly that she could stay.

If, in his comparatively sober moments, the memory of Madeleine intruded, he cast it out with a curse. Not because he blamed her for his downfall; he blamed no one but himself; but because any recollection of the past, all it had been and promised, was unendurable. Whether he had been strong or weak in electing to go straight to perdition when Life had scourged him, he neither knew nor cared. He began to drink on the steamer, determined to forget for the present, at least; but the mental condition induced was far more agreeable than those moments of sobriety when he felt as if he were in hell with fire in his vitals and cold terror of the future in his brain. In New York, driven by his pride, he had made one or two attempts to recover himself, but the writing of unsigned editorials on subjects that interested him not at all was like wandering in a thirsty desert without an oasis in sight - after the champagne of his life in San Francisco with a future as glittering as its skies at night and the daily companionship of a woman whom he had believed the fates must give him wholly in time.

He finally renounced self-respect as a game not worth the candle. Moreover, the clarity of mind necessary to sustained work embraced ever the image of Madeleine; what he had lost and what he had never possessed.

And, again, he tormented himself with imaginings of her own suffering and despair; alternated with visions of Madeleine enthroned, secure, impeccable, admired, envied - and with other men in love with her! Some depth of insight convinced him that she loved him immortally, but he knew her need for mental companionship, and the thought that she might find it, however briefly and barrenly, with another man, sent him plunging once more.

His friends and admirers on the newspaper staffs had been loyal, but not only was he irritated by their manifest attempts to reclaim him, but he grew to hate them as so many accusing reminders of the great gifts he was striving to blast out by the roots; and, finding it difficult to avoid them, he had, as soon as he was put in possession of his small income, deliberately transferred himself to the Five Points, where they would hardly be likely to trace him, certainly not to seek his society.

And, on the whole, this experience in a degraded and perilous quarter, famous the world over as a degree or two worse than any pest-hole of its kind, was the most enjoyable of his prolonged debauch. It was only a few yards from Broadway, but he had never set foot in that magnificent thoroughfare of brown stone and white marble, aristocratic business partner of Fifth Avenue, since he entered a precinct so different from New York, as his former world knew it, that he might have been on a convict island in the South Seas.

The past never obtruded itself here. He was surrounded by danger and degradation, ugliness unmitigated, and a complete indifference to anything in the world but vice, crime, liquor and the primitive appetites. Even the children in the swarming squalid streets looked like little old men and women; they fought in the gutters for scraps of refuse, or stood staring sullenly before them, the cry in their emaciated bodies dulled with the poisons of malnutrition; or making quick passes at the pocket of a thief. The girls had never been young, never worn anything but rags or mean finery, the boys were in training for a career of crime, the sodden women seemed to have no natural affection for the young they bore as lust prompted. Men beat their wives or strumpets with no interference from the police. The Sixth Ward was the worst on Manhattan, and the police had enough to do without wasting their time in this congested mass of the city's putrid dregs; who would be conferring a favor on the great and splendid and envied City of New York if they exterminated one another in a grand final orgy of blood and hate.

The irony in Masters' mind might sleep when that proud and contemptuous organ was sodden, but it was deathless. When he thought at all it was to congratulate himself with a laugh that he had found the proper setting for the final exit of a man whom Life had equipped to conquer, and Fate, in her most ironic mood, had challenged to battle; with the sting of death in victory if he won. He had beaten her at her own game. He had always aimed at consummation, the masterpiece; and here, in his final degradation, he had accomplished it.

This morning he laughed aloud, and the woman - or girl? - her body was young but her scarred face was almost aged - wondered if he were going mad at last. There was little time lost in the Five Points upon discussion of personal peculiarities, but all took for granted that this man was half mad and would be wholly so before long.

"Is anything the matter?" she asked timidly, her eye on the door but not daring to bolt.

"Oh, no, nothing! Nothing in all this broad and perfect world. Life is a sweet-scented garden where all the good are happy and all the bad receive their just and immediate deserts. You are the complete epitome of life, yourself, and I gaze upon you with a satisfaction as complete. I wouldn't change you for the most silken and secluded beauty in Bleecker Street, and you may stay here for ever. The more hideous you become the more pleased I shall be. And you needn't be afraid I have gone mad. I am damnably sane. And still more damnably sober. Go out and buy me a bottle of Lethe, and be quick about it. This is nearly finished."

"Do you mean rum?" She was reassured, somewhat, but he had a fashion of making what passed for her brain feel as if it had been churned.

"Yes, I mean rum, damn you. Clear out."

He opened an old wallet and threw a handful of bills on the floor. "Go round into Broadway and buy yourself a gown of white satin and a wreath of lilies for your hair. You would be a picture to make the angels weep, while I myself wept from pure joy. Get out."

XLIII

Madeleine had forced herself to eat a light dinner, and a few minutes before eleven she drank a cup of strong coffee; but when she entered upon the sights and sounds and stenches of Worth Street she nearly fainted.

The night was hot. The narrow crooked streets of the Five Points were lit with gas that shone dimly through the grimy panes of the lamp posts or through the open doors of groggeries and fetid shops. The gutter was a sewer. Probably not one of those dehumanized creatures ever bathed. Some of the children were naked and all looked as if they had been dipped in the gutters and tossed out to dry. The streets swarmed with them; and with men and women between the ages of sixteen and forty. One rarely lived longer than that in the Five Points. Some were shrieking and fighting, others were horribly quiet. Men and women lay drunk in the streets or hunched against the dripping walls, their mouths with black teeth or no teeth hanging loosely, their faces purple or pallid. Screams came from one of the tenements, but neither of the two detectives escorting the party turned his head.

Madeleine had imagined nothing like this. Her only acquaintance with vice had been in the dens and dives of San Francisco, and she had pictured something of the same sort intensified. But there was hardly a point of resemblance. San Francisco has always had a genius for making vice picturesque. The outcasts of the rest of the world do their worst and let it go at that. Moreover, in San Francisco she had never seen poverty. There was work for all, there were no beggars, no hungry tattered children, no congested districts. Vice might be an agreeable resource but it was forced on no one; and always the atmosphere of its indulgence was gay. She had witnessed scenes of riotous drunkenness, but there was something debonair about even those bent upon extermination, either of an antagonist or the chandeliers and glass-ware, and she had never seen men sodden save on the water front. Even then they were often grinning.

But this looked like plain Hell to Madeleine, or worse. The Hell of the Bible and Dante had a lively accompaniment of writhing flames and was presumably clean. This might be an underground race condemned to a sordid filthy and living death for unimaginable crimes of a previous existence. Even the children looked as if they had come back to Earth with the sins of threescore and ten stamped upon their weary wicked faces. Madeleine's strong soul faltered, and she grasped Holt's arm.

"Well, you see for yourself," he said unsympathetically. "Better go back and let me bring him to you. One of our men can easily knock him out -"

"I'm here and I shall go on. I'll stay all night if necessary."

Lacey looked at her with open adoration; he had fallen truculently in love with her. If Masters no longer loved her he felt quite equal to killing him, although with no dreams for himself. He hoped that if Masters were too far gone for redemption she would recognize the fact at once, forget him, and find happiness somewhere. He was glad on the whole that she had come to Five Points.

"What's the program?" asked one of the detectives, kicking a sprawling form out of the way. "Do you know where he hangs out?"

"No," said Lacey. "He seems to go where fancy leads. We'll have to go from one groggery to another, and then try the dance houses, unless they pass the word in time. The police are supposed to have closed them, you know."

"Yes, they have!" The man's hearty Irish laugh startled these wretched creatures, unused to laughter, and they forsook their apathy or belligerence for a moment to stare. "They simply moved to the back, or to the cellar. They know we believe in lettin' 'em go to the devil their own way. Might as well turn in here."

They entered one of the groggeries. It was a large room. The ceiling was low. The walls were foul with the accumulations of many years, it was long since the tables had been washed. The bar, dripping and slimy, looked as if about to fall to pieces, and the drinks were served in cracked mugs. The bar-tender was evidently an ex-prize-fighter, but the loose skin, empty of muscle, hung from his bare arms in folds. The air was dense with vile tobacco smoke, adding to the choice assortment of stenches imported from without and conferred by Time within. Men and women, boys and girls, sat at the tables drinking, or lay on the floor. There they would remain until their drunken stupor wore off, when they would stagger home to begin a new day. A cracked fiddle was playing. The younger people and some of the older were singing in various keys. Many were drinking solemnly as if drinking were a ritual. Others were grinning with evident enjoyment and a few were hilarious.

The party attracted little general attention. Investigating travellers, escorted by detectives, had visited the Five Points more than once, curious to see in what way it justified its reputation for supremacy over the East End of London and the Montmartre of Paris; and although pockets usually were picked, no violence was offered if the detectives maintained a bland air of detachment. They did not even resent the cologne-drenched handkerchiefs the visitors invariably held to their noses. As evil odors meant nothing to them, they probably mistook the gesture for modesty.

Madeleine preferred her smelling salts, and at Holt's suggestion had wrapped her handkerchief about the gold and crystal bottle. But she forgot the horrible atmosphere as she peered into the face of every man who might be Masters. She wore a plain black dress and a small black hat, but her beauty was difficult to obscure. Her cheeks were white and her brown eyes had lost their sparkle long since, but men not too drunk to notice a lovely woman or her manifest close scrutiny, not only leered up into her face but would have jerked her down beside them had it not been for their jealous partners and the presence of the detectives. There was a rumor abroad that the new City Administration intended to seek approval if not fame by cleaning out the Five Points, tearing down the wretched tenements and groggeries, and scattering its denizens; and none was too reckless not to be on his guard against a calamity which would deprive him not only of all he knew of pleasure but of an almost impregnable refuge after crime.

The women, bloated, emaciated with disease, few with any pretension to looks or finery, made insulting remarks as Madeleine examined their partners, or stared at her in a sort of terrible wonder. She had no eyes for them. When she reached the end of the room, looking down into the faces of the men she was forced to step over, she turned and methodically continued her pilgrimage up another lane between the tables.

"Good God!" exclaimed Holt to Lacey. "There he is! I hoped we should have to visit at least twenty of these hells, and that she'd faint or give up."

"How on earth can you distinguish any one in this infernal smoke?"

"Got the eyes of a cat. There he is - in that corner by the door. God! What a female thing he's got with him."

"Hope it'll cure her - and that we can get out of this pretty soon. Strange things are happening within me."

There was an uproar on the other side of the room. One man had made up his mind to follow this fair visitor, and his woman was beating him in the face, shrieking her curses.

A party of drunken sailors staggered in, singing uproariously, and almost fell over the bar.

But not a sound had penetrated Madeleine's unheeding ears. She had seen Masters.

His drab had not taken his invitation to bedeck herself too literally, nor had she ventured into Broadway. But after returning with the rum she had gone as far as Fell Street and bought herself all the tawdry finery her funds would command. She wore it with tipsy pride: a pink frock of slazy silk with as full a flowing skirt as any on Fifth Avenue during the hour of promenade, a green silk mantle, and a hat as flat as a plate trimmed with faded roses, soiled streamers hanging down over her impudent chignon. She was attracting far more attention than the simply dressed lady from the upper world. The eyes of the women in her vicinity were redder with envy than with liquor and they cursed her shrilly. One of the younger women, carried away by a sudden dictation of femininity, made a dart for the fringed mantle with obvious intent to appropriate it by force. She received a blow in the face from the dauntless owner that sent her sprawling, while the others mingled jeers with their curses.

Masters was leaning on the table, supporting his head with his hands and laughing. He had passed the stage where he wanted to talk, but it would be morning before his brain would be completely befuddled.

Madeleine's body became so stiff that her heels left the floor and she stood on her toes. Holt and Lacey grasped her arms, but she did not sway; she stood staring at the man she had come for. There was little semblance of the polished, groomed, haughty man who had won her. His face was not swollen but it was a dark uniform red and the lines cut it to the bone. The slight frown he had always worn had deepened to an ugly scowl. His eyes were injected and dull, his hair was turning gray. His mouth that he had held in such firm curves was loose and his teeth stained. She remembered how his teeth had flashed when he smiled, the extraordinary brilliancy of his gray eyes.... The groggery vanished ... they were sitting before the fire in the Occidental Hotel....

The daze and the vision lasted only a moment. She disengaged herself from her escorts and walked rapidly toward the table.

Gertrude Atherton

XLIV

Masters did not recognize her at once. Her face lay buried deep in his mind, covered with the debris of innumerable carouses, forgotten women, and every defiance he had been able to fling in the face of the civilization he had been made to adorn. As she stood quite still looking at him he had a confused idea that she was a Madonna, and his mind wandered to churches he had attended on another planet, where pretty fashionable women had commanded his escort. Then he began to laugh again. The idea of a Madonna in a groggery of the Five Points was more amusing than the fracas just over.

"Langdon!" she said imperiously. "Don't you know me?"

Then he recognized her, but he believed she was a ghost. He had had delirium tremens twice, and this no doubt was a new form. He gave a shaking cry and shrank back, his hands raised with the palms outward.

"Curse you!" he screamed. "It's not there. I *don't* see you!"

He extended one of his trembling hands, still with his horrified eyes on the apparition, filled his mug from a bottle and drank the liquor off with a gulp. Then he flung the mug to the floor and staggered to his feet, his eyes roving to the men behind her. "What does this mean?" he stammered. "Are you here or aren't you - dead or alive?"

"We're here all right," said Holt, in his matter-of-fact voice. "And this really is she. She has come for you."

"Come for me - for me!" His roar of laughter was drunken but its note was even more ironic than when his mirth had been excited by the mean drama of the women. He fell back in his chair for he was unable to stand. "Well, go back where you came from. There's nothing here for you. Tout passe, tout lasse, tout casse.... Here - what's your name?" he said brutally to his companion. "Go and get me another mug."

But the young woman, who had been gaping at the scene, suddenly recovered herself. She ran round the table and flung her arms about his neck. "He's my man!" she shrieked. "You can't have him." And she sputtered obscenities.

Madeleine reached over, tore her from Masters, dragged her across the table, whirled her about, and flung her to the floor. The neighborhood shrieked its delight. The rest of the room took no notice of them. The drunken sailors were still singing and many took up the refrain.

"No," said Madeleine. "He's mine and I'll have him."

"Now I know you are not Madeleine," cried Masters furiously, and trying to rise again. "She never was your sort, you damned whore, to fight over a man in a groggery. She was a lady -"

"She was also a woman," said Madeleine coolly. "And never more so than now. You are coming with me."

"I'll see you in hell first."

"Well, I'll go there with you if you like. But you'll come home with me first."

"Even if you were she, I've no use for you, I'd forgotten your existence. If I'd remembered you at all it was to curse you. I'll never - never - " His voice trailed off although his eyes still held their look of hard contempt.

His companion had pulled herself to her feet with the aid of an empty chair. She made a sudden dart at Madeleine, her claws extended, recognizing a far more formidable rival than the harlot she had hammered and displaced. But Madeleine had not forgotten to give her the corner of an eye. She caught the threatening arm in her strong hand, twisted it nearly from its socket, and the woman with a wild shriek of pain collapsed once more.

Masters began to laugh again, then broke off abruptly and began to shudder violently. He stared as if the nightmare of his terrible years were racing across his vision.

"Now," said Madeleine. "I've fought for you on your own field and won you. You are mine. Come."

"I'll come," he mumbled. He tried to rise but fell back. "I'm very drunk," he said apologetically. "Sorry."

He made no resistance as Holt and Lacey took him by

his arms and supported him out of the groggery and out of the Five Points to a waiting hack; Madeleine and the detectives forming a body-guard in the rear.

XLV

It was two months before Madeleine saw him again. He was installed in his room, two powerful nurses attended him day and night, and Holt slept on a cot near the bed. He was almost ungovernable at first, in spite of the drugs the doctor gave him, but these had their effect in time; and then the tapering-off process began, combined with hotly peppered soups and the vegetable most inimical to alcohol; finally food in increasing quantity to restore his depleted vitality. In his first sane moment he had made Holt promise that Madeleine should not see him, and she had sent word that she would wait until he sent for her.

Madeleine took long walks, and drives, and read in the Astor Library. She also replenished her wardrobe. The color came back to her cheeks, the sparkle to her eyes. She had made all her plans. The house in Virginia was being renovated. She would take him there as soon as he could be moved. When he was strong again he would start his newspaper. Holt and Lacey were as overjoyed at the prospect of being his assistant editors as at the almost unbelievable rescue of Langdon Masters.

He had remained in bed after the worst was over, sunk in torpor, with no desire to leave it or to live. But strength gradually returned to his wasted frame, the day nurse was dismissed, and he appeared to listen when Holt talked to him, although he would not reply. One day, however, when he believed himself to be alone, he opened his eyes and stared at the wall covered with his books, as he had done before through half-closed lids. Then his gaze wandered to the green curtains. But his mind was clear. He was visited by no delusions. This was not the Occidental Hotel.

It was long since he had read a book! He wondered, with his first symptom of returning interest in life, if he was strong enough to cross the room and find one of his favorite volumes. But as he raised himself on his elbow Holt bent over him.

"What is it, old fellow?"

"Those books? How did they get here?"

"Lacey brought them. You remember, you left them in the *Times* cellar."

"Are these your rooms?"

"No, they are Madeleine Talbot's."

He made no reply, but he did not scowl and turn his back as he had done whenever Holt had tentatively mentioned her name before. The sight of his familiar beloved books had softened his harsh spirit, and the hideous chasm between his present and his past seemed visibly shrinking. His tones, however, had not softened when he asked curtly after a moment:

"What is the meaning of it all? Why is she here? Is Talbot dead?"

"No, he divorced her."

"Divorced her? Madeleine?" He almost sat upright. Mrs. Abbott could not have looked more horrified. "Is this some infernal joke?"

"Are you strong enough to hear the whole story? I warn you it isn't a pretty one. But I've promised her I would tell you -"

"What did he divorce her for?"

"Desertion. There was worse behind."

"Do you mean to tell me there was another man? I'll break your neck."

"There was no other man. I'll give you a few drops of digitalis, although you must have the heart of an ox -"

"Give me a drink. I'm sick of your damn physic. Don't worry. I'm out of that, and I shan't go back."

Holt poured him out a small quantity of old Bourbon and diluted it with water. Masters regarded it with a look of scorn but tossed it off.

"What was the worse behind?"

"When she heard what had become of you - she got it out of me - she deliberately made a drunkard of herself. She became the scandal of the town. She was cast out, neck and crop. Every friend she ever had cut her, avoided her as if she were a leper. She left the doctor and lived by herself in one room on the Plaza. I met her again in one of the worst dives in

San Francisco -"

"Stop!" Masters' voice rose to a scream. He tried to get out of bed but fell back on the pillows. "You are a liar - you - you -"

"You shall listen whether you relish the facts or not. I have given her my promise." And he told the story in all its abominable details, sparing the writhing man on the bed nothing. He drew upon his imagination for scenes between Madeleine and the doctor, of whose misery he gave a harrowing picture. He described the episode on the boat after her drinking bout at Blazes', of the futile attempts of Sally Abbott and Talbot to cure her. He gave graphic and hideous pictures of the dives she had frequented alone, the risks she had run in the most vicious resorts on Barbary Coast. Not until he had seared Masters' brain indelibly did he pass to Madeleine's gradual rise from her depths, the restoration of her beauty and charm and sanity. It was when she was almost herself again that Talbot had offered to forgive her and take her to Europe to live, offering divorce as the alternative.

"Of course she accepted the divorce," Holt concluded. "That meant freedom to go to you."

Masters had grown calm by degrees. "I should never have dreamed even Madeleine was capable of that," he said. "And there was a time when I believed there was no height to which she could not soar. She is a great woman and a great lover, and I am no more worthy of her now than I was in that sink where you found me. Nor ever shall be. Go out and bring in a barber."

Holt laughed. "At least you are yourself again and I

fancy she'll ask no more than that. Shall I tell her you will see her in an hour?"

"Yes, I'll see her. God! What a woman."

XLVI

Madeleine made her toilette with trembling hands, nevertheless with no detail neglected. Her beautiful chestnut hair was softly parted and arranged in a mass of graceful curls at the back of the head. She wore a house-gown of white muslin sprigged with violets, and a long Marie Antoinette fichu, pale green and diaphanous. Where it crossed she fastened a bunch of violets. She looked like a vision of spring, a grateful vision for a sick room.

When Holt tapped on her door on his way out the second time, muttering characteristically: "Coast clear. All serene," she walked down the hall with nothing of the primitive fierce courage she had exhibited in Five Points. She was terrified at the ordeal before her, afraid of appearing sentimental and silly; that he would find her less beautiful than his memory of her, or gone off and no longer desirable. What if he should die suddenly? Holt had told her of his agitation. This visit should have been postponed until he had slept and recuperated. She had sent him word to that effect but he had replied that he had no intention of waiting.

She stood still for a few moments until she felt calmer, then turned the knob of Masters' door and walked in.

He was sitting propped up in bed and she had an

agreeable shock of surprise. In spite of all efforts of will her imagination had persisted in picturing him with a violent red face and red injected eyes, a loose sardonic mouth and lines like scars. His face was very pale, his eyes clear and bright, his hair trimmed in its old close fashion, his mouth grimly set. Although he was very thin the lines in his cheeks were less pronounced. He looked years older, of course, and the life he had led had set its indelible seal upon him, but he was Langdon Masters again nevertheless.

His eyes dilated when he saw her, but he smiled whimsically.

"So you want what is left of this battered old husk, Madeleine?" he asked. "You in the prime of your beauty and your youth! Better think it over."

She smiled a little, too.

"Do you mean that?"

"No, I don't! Come here! Come here!"

XLVII

In the winter of 1878-79 Mrs. Ballinger gave a luncheon in honor of Mrs. McLane, who had arrived in San Francisco the day before after a long visit in Europe. The city was growing toward the west, but Ballinger House still looked like an outpost on its solitary hill and was almost surrounded by a grove of eucalyptus trees.

Mrs. Abbott grumbled as she always did at the long journey, skirting far higher hills, and through sand dunes still unsubdued by man and awaiting the first dry wind of summer to transform themselves into clouds of dust. But a sand storm would not have kept her away. The others invited were her daughter-in-law, who had met Mrs. McLane at Sacramento, Guadalupe Hathaway, now Mrs. Ogden Bascom, Mrs. Montgomery, Mrs. Yorba, whose husband had recently built the largest and ugliest house in San Francisco, perched aloft on Nob Hill; several more of Mrs. McLane's favorites, old and young, and Maria Groome, born Ballinger, now a proud pillar of San Francisco Society.

The dining-room of Ballinger House was long and narrow and from its bow window commanded a view of the Bay. It was as uncomely with its black walnut furniture and brown walls as the rest of that aristocratic abode, across whose threshold no loose fish had ever darted; but its dingy walls were more or less concealed by paintings of the martial Virginia ancestors of Mrs. Ballinger and her husband, the table linen had been woven for her in Ireland, the cut glass blown for her in England; the fragile china came from Sevres, and the massive silver had travelled from England to Virginia in the reign of Elizabeth. The room may have been ugly, nay, ponderous, but it had an air!

The women who graced the board were dressed, with one or two exceptions, in the height of the mode. Save Maria Groome each had made at least one trip to Europe and left her measurements with Worth. Maria did not begin her pilgrimages to Europe until the eighties, and then it was old carved furniture she brought home; dress she always held in disdain, possibly because her husband's mistresses were ever attired in the excess of the fashion.

Mrs. Ballinger was now in her fifties but still one of the most beautiful women in San Francisco; and she still wore shining gray gowns that matched the bright silver of her hair to a shade. Her descendants had inherited little of her beauty (Alexina Groome as yet roaming space, and, no doubt, having her subtle way with ghosts old and new).

Mrs. McLane had discharged commissions for every woman present except Maria, and their gowns had been unpacked on the moment, that they might be displayed at this notable function. They wore the new long basque and overskirt made of cloth or cashmere, combined with satin, velvet or brocade, and with the exception of Mrs. Abbott they had removed their hats. Chignons had disappeared. Hair was elaborately dressed at the back or arranged in high puffs with two long curls suspended. Marguerite Abbott and Annette wore the new plaids. Mrs. Abbott had graduated from black satin and bugles to cloth, but her bonnet was of jet.

"Now!" exclaimed Mrs. McLane, who had been plied with eager questions from oysters to dessert. "I've told you all the news about the fashions, the salon, the plays, the opera, all the scandals of Paris I can remember but you'll never guess my *piece de resistance*."

"What - what - " Tea was forgotten.

"Well - as you know, I was in Berlin during the Congress -"

"Did you see Bismark - Disraeli -"

"I did and met them. But they are not of half as much interest to you as some one else - two people - I met."

"But who?"

"Can't you guess?"

"I know!" cried Guadalupe Bascom. "Langdon and Madeleine Masters."

"No! What would they be doing in Berlin?" demanded Mrs. Ballinger. "I thought he was editing some paper in New York."

"'Lupie has guessed correctly. It's evident that you don't keep up. We're just the same old stick-in-the-muds. 'Lupie, how did you guess? I'll wager you never see a New York newspaper yourself."

"Not I. But one does hear a little Eastern news now and again. I happen to know that Masters has made a success of his paper and it would be just like him to go to the Congress of Berlin. What was he doing there?"

"Oh, nothing in particular. Merely corresponding with his paper, and, in the eyes of many, eclipsing Blowitz."

"Who is Blowitz?"

"Mon dieu! Mon dieu! But after all London is farther off than New York, and I don't fancy you read the *Times* when you are there - which is briefly and seldom. Paris is our Mecca. Well, Blowitz -"

"But Madeleine? Madeleine? It is about her we want to hear. What do we care about tiresome political letters in solemn old newspapers? How did she look? How dressed? Was she ahead of the mode as ever? Does she look much older? Does she show what she has been through.... Oh, Antoinette - Mrs. McLane - Mamma - how tiresome you are!"

Mrs. Abbott had not joined in this chorus. She had emitted a series of grunts - no less primitive word expressing her vocal emissions when disgusted. She now had four chins, her eyes were alarmingly protuberant, and her face, what with the tight lacing in vogue, much good food and wine, and a pious disapproval of powder or any care of a complexion which should remain as God made it, was of a deep mahogany tint; but her hand still held the iron rod, and if its veins had risen its muscles had never grown flaccid.

"Abominable!" she ejaculated when she could make herself heard. "To think that a man and a woman like that should be rewarded by fame and prosperity. They were thoroughly bad and should have been punished accordingly."

"Oh, no, they were not bad, ma chere," said Mrs. McLane lightly. "They were much too good. That was the whole trouble. And you must admit that for their temporary fall from grace they were sufficiently punished, poor things."

"Antoinette, I am surprised." Mrs. Ballinger spoke as severely as Mrs. Abbott. She looked less the Southerner for the moment than the Puritan. "They disgraced both themselves and Society. I was glad to hear of their reform, but they should have continued to live in sackcloth for the rest of their lives. For such to enjoy happiness and success is to shake the whole social structure, and it is a blow to the fundamental laws of religion and morality."

"But perhaps they are not happy, mamma." Maria spoke hopefully, although the fates seemed to have nothing in pickle for her erratic mate. "Mrs. McLane has not yet told us -"

"Oh, but they are! Quite the happiest couple I have ever seen, and likely to remain so. That's a case of true love if ever there was one. I mislaid my skepticism all the time I was in Berlin - a whole month!"

"Abominable!" rumbled Mrs. Abbott. "And when I think of poor Howard - dead of apoplexy -"

"Howard ate too much, was too fond of Burgundy, and

grew fatter every year. Madeleine could reclaim Masters, but she never had any influence over Howard."

"Well, she could have waited -"

"Masters was pulled up in the nick of time. A year more of that horrible life he was leading and he would have been either unreclaimable or dead. It makes me believe in Fate - and I am a good Churchwoman."

"It's a sad world," commented Mrs. Ballinger with a sigh. "I confess I don't understand it. When I think of Sally -"

Mrs. Montgomery, a good kind woman, whose purse was always open to her less fortunate friends, shook her head. "I do not like such a sequel. I agree with Alexina and Charlotte. They disgraced themselves and our proud little Society; they should have been more severely punished. Possibly they will be."

"I doubt it," said Mrs. Bascom drily. "And not only because I am a woman of the world and have looked at life with both eyes open, but because Masters had success in him. I'll wager he's had his troubles all in one great landslide. And Madeleine was born to be some man's poem. The luxe binding got badly torn and stained, but no doubt she's got a finer one than ever, and is unchanged - or even improved - inside."

"Oh, do let me get in a word edgeways," cried young Mrs. Abbott. "Tell me, Mamma - what does Madeleine look like? Has she lost her beauty?"

"She looked to me more beautiful than ever. I'd vow

Masters thinks so."

"Has she wrinkles? Lines?"

"Not one. Have we grown old since she left us? It's not so many years ago?"

"Oh, I know. But after all she went through.... How was she dressed?"

"What are her favorite colors?"

"Who makes her gowns?"

"Has she as much elegance and style as ever?"

"Did she get her mother's jewels? Did she wear them in Berlin?"

"Is she in Society there? Is her grand air as noticeable among all those court people as it was here?"

"Oh, mamma, mamma, you are so tiresome!"

Mrs. McLane had had time to drink a second cup of tea.

"My head spins. Where shall I begin? The gowns she wore in Berlin were made at Worth's. Where else? She still wears golden-brown, and amber, and green - sometimes azure - blue at night. She looked like a fairy queen in blue gauze and diamond stars in her hair one night at the American Legation -"

"How does she wear her hair?"

"There she is not so much a la mode. She has studied her own style, and has found several ways of dressing it that become her - sometimes in a low coil, almost on her neck, sometimes on top of her head in a braid like a coronet, sometimes in a soft psyche knot. There never was anything monotonous about Madeleine."

"I'm going to try every one tomorrow. Has she any children?"

"One. She left him at their place in Virginia. I saw his picture. A beauty, of course."

Mrs. Ballinger raised her pencilled eyebrows and glanced at Maria. Mrs. Abbott gave a deep rumbling groan.

"Poor Howard!"

"He dreed his weird," said Mrs. McLane indifferently. "He couldn't help it. Neither could Madeleine."

"Well, I'd like to hear something more about Langdon Masters," announced Guadalupe Bascom. "That is, if you have all satisfied your curiosity about Madeleine's clothes. He is the one man I never could twist around my finger and I've never forgotten him. How does he look? He certainly should carry some stamp of the life he led."

"Oh, he looks older, of course, and he has deeper lines and some gray hairs. But he's thin, at least. His figure did not suffer if his face did - somewhat. He looks even more interesting - at least women would think so. You know we good women always have a fatal weakness for the man who has lived too much."

"Speak for yourself, Antoinette." Mrs. Ballinger looked like an effigy of virtue in silver. "And at your age you should be ashamed to utter such a sentiment even if you felt it."

"My hair may be as white as yours," rejoined Mrs. McLane tartly. "But I remain a woman, and for that reason attract men to this day."

"Is Masters as brilliant as ever - in conversation, I mean? Is he gay? Lively?"

"I cannot say that I found him gay, and I really saw very little of him except at functions. He was very busy. But Mr. McLane was with him a good deal, and said that although he was rather grim and quiet at times, at others he was as brilliant as his letters."

"Does he drink at all, or is he forced to be a teetotaller?"

"Not a bit of it. He drinks at table as others do; no more, no less."

"Then he is cured," said Mrs. Bascom contentedly. "Well, I for one am glad that it's all right. Still, if he had fallen in love with me he would have remained an eminent citizen - without a hideous interval he hardly can care to recall - and become the greatest editor in California. Have they any social position in New York?"

"Probably. I did not ask. They hardly looked like outcasts. You must remember their story is wholly unknown in fashionable New York. Scarcely any one here knows any one in New York Society; or has time

Gertrude Atherton

for it when passing through.... But I don't fancy they care particularly for Society. In Berlin, whenever it was possible, they went off by themselves. But of course it was necessary for both to go in Society there, and she must have been able to help him a good deal."

"European Society! I suppose she'll be presented to the Queen of England next! - But no! Thank heaven she can't be. Good Queen Victoria is as rigid about divorce as we are. Nor shall she ever cross my threshold if she returns here." And Mrs. Abbott scalded herself with her third cup of tea and emitted terrible sounds.

Mrs. Yorba, a tall, spare, severe-looking woman, who had taught school in New England in her youth, and never even powdered her nose, spoke for the first time. Her tones were slow and portentous, as became one who, owing to her unfortunate nativity, had sailed slowly into this castellated harbor, albeit on her husband's golden ship.

"We may no longer have it in our power to punish Mrs. Langdon Masters," she said. "But at least we shall punish others who violate our code, even as we have done in the past. San Francisco Society shall always be a model for the rest of the world."

"I hope so!" cried Mrs. McLane. "But the world has a queer fashion of changing and moving."

Mrs. Ballinger rose. "I have no misgivings for the future of our Society, Antoinette McLane. Our grandchildren will uphold the traditions we have created, for our children will pass on to them our own immutable laws. Shall we go into the front parlor? I do so want to show it to you. I have a new set of blue satin damask and a crystal chandelier."